Under the Weeping Willow

Kay Lewis

authorHOUSE®

AuthorHouse™
1663 Liberty Drive
Bloomington, IN 47403
www.authorhouse.com
Phone: 1 (800) 839-8640

Published by AuthorHouse 06/26/2018

ISBN: 978-1-5462-4479-0 (sc)
ISBN: 978-1-5462-4478-3 (e)

Library of Congress Control Number: 2018906848

Print information available on the last page.

Dedication

Dear Mother,

I wrote this story for you. It was written so
you would finally believe that your daughters'
strength and grace come from you.

Contents

Acknowledgments

I would like to thank Author House for giving me
the chance to share my story and bring my vision to
life. Without the diligence, patience, and expertise
of a professional team, my readers would not be
able to enjoy what I believe to be an enthralling
tale of a family's struggle and triumph.

Also, to my family and friends, thank you for your support
and confidence in me. From helping me to develop
the characters, critiquing when needed, and putting
up with my madness on seemingly endless nights;
your love is priceless.

Prologue

I was told that it was planted just for me - planted when I was born, and meant to be a reminder of my birth- a comforting friend throughout my young years. Why my grandfather decided to get up one day and say, "I think I'm going to plant a tree for my grandbaby today" is beyond me. Why he chose this particular tree also eludes me, but I am ever so grateful that he chose such a regal creature to watch over me. I have lost count of how many times I climbed those branches to hide from ¬sharp tongues and prying eyes. It was as if it could sense the evil approaching as its thick foliage would bend towards me to keep me safer. How many times have I dared myself to climb higher and higher proving to myself, and to a world that wasn't watching me at the moment, that I was brave? No matter what they thought but wouldn't say, I was determined to make it to the top. It has shaded me on scorching hot days when no matter how much I begged, no one would let me past the screen door. Forced to quench my thirst from the water hose conveniently placed on the side of the old house, I would settle under the cool branches, hanging low like soft green feathers and lose myself in the shade. The most cherished times, however, were the evenings when the sky looked like an artist's swift strokes with a medley of soft colors. The breeze would whip through the leaves, enveloping me in calmness. I would sit there thoroughly enjoying my own company until I heard the loud high-pitched voice of my mother cutting through my senses like a knife, demanding that I come inside for supper. My tree has witnessed laughter from get-togethers with family and friends sharing delicious seafood, hoola-hoop contests, and foot races. It has seen catfights between sisters and flared tempers amongst brothers. It is no stranger to children riding by on their bicycles, supped-up cars revving engines in the driveway, or motorcycle wipeouts on the side of the road. But it has also witnessed other moments; darker moments. These are moments that brought shame to the spirit as well as anger, hurt, resentment, and callousness, all witnessed by the best secret keeper of all.

The Beginning

"Please Lord, let my baby make it." Lynette was lying in Richmond City Memorial Hospital. She had been crying and praying non-stop since she arrived through the hospital's emergency doors a few hours earlier. One minute she was hanging the sheets out on the clothes-line, and the next minute she was hit with a horrific pain in her stomach. She was only five months along and she knew that something had gone terribly wrong. She quickly called her older sister, Lynda who had arrived within minutes to take her to the hospital.

Now, as she lay in the hard hospital bed, her only thoughts were that she may never see her baby alive. She had longed for something of her own; something that she wouldn't have to share with anyone else. A little girl was all she could think about. She dreamed of dressing her up like a doll baby, like she used to do when she was a little girl. Lynette was only eighteen, and being the youngest of ten children, she was everyone's child. She had grown up to be a good girl, not only due to her parents' disciplinary measures, but as a result of those of her brothers and sisters as well. Also, being the youngest had always made her a target for her eldest brothers who were definitely big and strong due to chopping wood since they took their first steps. They (Lynette and her siblings) had been born and raised in Henrico County just outside of Richmond City. Such a playful lot, they would toss her back and forth like a hot potato, ignoring her screams to stop.

"Put me down!" Lynette, very light-skinned, had turned beet red.

"Oh, gal shut up. You'll be alright!" The oldest brother Anthony would retort as he tossed her to his younger brother Bobby.

This would go on until their mother, Liz, came outside with the broom in her hand, and everyone would flee.

"Come on baby and help mama with these blackberry cobblers. I'll even let you have your own 'lil special bowl of berries all to yourself."

"Ooooooh. I love blackberries mama!" Lynette would squeal. She always loved those special moments when she could have her mama all to herself. She was always patient with her, while teaching her how to iron ribbons and sew clothes for her dolls. Her three older sisters always got to help their mom cook, but Lynette, at seven years old, was still too young to help with cooking anything too big.

Her father was an entirely different story. He was as mean as a snake. The only one who could put him in his place was his wife. He'd come home after losing in a poker game, cursing, drinking, and ordering everyone out of his house.

"Errbody get the hell outta my house!" Andrew would slur as he kicked open the screen door to the kitchen, spilling White Lighting Moonshine all over the floor, and tripping over the threshold as he came in. All the children would back up, eyes big as saucers, as their father advance on them.

"Drew what are you going on about now." Liz had come from the den where she had been folding laundry.

"I said I w-w-w-w-want eerrrrbody out of my god-dammed house!"

"Stop talking crazy, Drew. Lynette's only seven. Where is she going to go?"

"I don't give a damn how old she is! She can go get a job and help pay summa these damn bills around here!"

And this would go on for a little while until Andrew would stagger into the bedroom and pass out on the bed with his clothes on. His steady snores afterwards would bring out a breath of relief from the worried kids.

Lynette, all grown up, was now waiting for the nurse to come in and give her the prognosis of her baby. She hears voices outside her door and closes her eyes in anticipation. When she opens them, there is a pleasant looking nurse smiling at her as she closes the door behind her.

"Miss Lee, how are you feeling?"

"Better. Thank you." Lynette was too scared of the answer she would get if she asked about her baby.

The nurse seemed to sense this. "I have good news about your baby." We ran some blood tests and it looks like your baby is going to be just fine. We thought that your body may have been rejecting it, but it turns out that it's healthy."

As Lynette was thanking God for this miracle, the nurse leaned over her and whispered. "Would you like to know what the sex is? We're not supposed to tell, but I thought you might want to know."

Lynette shook her head up and down, still too stunned and relieved to speak.

"Congratulations. It's a girl."

First Chapter

"Netty!" A tall, plump, mocha-colored woman ran up the gravel driveway to the house. "Netty!" Rita called out again as she finally made it to the clothes-line where Lynette was hanging clothes. "Girl, yo daddy got that li'l girl of yours headed down Charles City and you know he's drunk!"

"What? I know you're lying." Lynette closed her eyes and said a silent prayer that her child was safe.

Andrew was known to have Ayanna almost to Charles City when he was drunk. He would simply lift her five-year-old body in the basket, put a fifth of gin in his pocket, and off they would go on an adventure. It was normal to see the duo weaving in and out of the road with Ayanna squealing with laughter.

"I don't know what I'm going do about that daddy of mine."

Lynette quickly ran across the field to retrieve her keys with Rita right on her heels. They then jumped into Lynette's red Mustang and took off down the road. She sped out of the driveway so fast that the gravel was now all over the front yard. They drove down Rt.5 for about 10 minutes when they finally spotted Andrew and Ayanna.

Sure enough, they were on the bike riding in the middle

of the road. Rita and Lynette could hear Ayanna yelling. "Wooooah! You got it granddaddy! Turn that way! Now turn this way! Yeeeeaah!" She squealed with delight and clapped her hands.

Lynette quickly swerved around her daughter and father and cut them off before they could ride any further. Unusual of a drunk, Andrew was amazingly quick and managed to stop right before he hit the Mustang.

"Gal are you crazy? You almost made me waste my good liquor. Not to mention I got li'l gal on the front of this here bike."

Andrew could barely hold his bike up with Ayanna wiggling to get out, but somehow, he managed.

Lynette, fury written all over her face, jumped out of the car and snatched her now stuck daughter out of the basket.

"What is wrong with you?" Lynette screamed, "Don't you know you could've killed my baby? I told you before not to be taking my baby all over the damn place!"

"I know that's right." Rita had now lifted her full-figured frame out of the small car and had plenty to say.

"You ought to be ashamed of yourself for having Ayanna out here like this. Any fool out here could have busted you upside your head and taken this child! It's a good thing that most of the folks around here know who you are."

As Rita and Lynette glared at Andrew, he decided to take another sip of his homemade moonshine. He then looked at Rita with watery eyes.

"Ain't nobody asked your hefty ass to say nothing. You know I ain't going to do nothing to hurt my baby. We were just going for a ride is all." Andrew slurred.

Rita put her hands on her ample hips and gave Andrew an icy stare.

"I was taught not to disrespect my elders so you're lucky. Stop taking this li'l girl all around the neighborhood when you been drinking."

"I ain't been drinki'n woman!" Andrew slurred as he took another sip from his bottle.

Rita just shook her head in disgust.

Meanwhile Lynette was busy getting Ayanna strapped in the backseat as fast as she could. She was relieved that Rita and she had found Ayanna and her father before anything bad had happened to them.

"Mama, what's pissy?"

"Huh?" Lynette asked, completely caught off guard.

"Granddaddy said that we were going out and get pissy." Ayanna confessed innocently.

Lynette could have choked her father to death if she could lay her hands on him at that moment. It was times like this that motivated her to work hard so she could afford to move out on her own.

"Don't worry about that baby. I'll explain later." Lynette said hoping Ayanna would forget the subject.

Meanwhile Rita and Andrew were still going at it. Andrew, however, was fast wearing down because of all the liquor he had consumed in the past few hours. He was now sweating like he was under a running shower and was looking defeated.

"Come on daddy. Come on and let's get you in the car." Lynette said as she walked over to Rita and her father and stood in between them like a referee.

Her father went with her obediently but could clearly be heard muttering.

"Gotdamn women. Always running off the mouth."

3

After everyone was safely in the Mustang with Andrew's bike sticking out of the hatchback, they took off back up Rt.5 towards home. Ayanna was busy making faces at her grandfather. He, on the other hand, had promptly passed out sleep with his head drooping over his chest.

"Netty, you need to keep a better eye on your daughter, my goddaughter, around your daddy. When are you going to be able to move you and your baby out of that house?" Rita chastised Lynette.

Lynette rolled her eyes. This was a conversation they had had on more than one occasion and Lynette was tired of it. She was doing the best she could, working at Safeway at night and driving school buses during the day while regular school was in session. It was the only way that she could be sure that errands were ran, bills were paid, and her daughter and father were properly taken care of.

Her mother had passed away three years ago, after losing a painful battle with cancer. Elizabeth had stayed vigilant until the day she took her last breath and went home to glory. Lynette was still feeling the pain from her loss. Her mother had always been her rock and Lynette seriously doubted that she could be as strong without her. Lord only knew how much she had been tested over the course of her life.

Lynette gave a long sigh.

"I'm working on it Rita. I just need a little time and a plan."

Rita sensed how tired Lynette was so she didn't say anything else for the remainder of the ride home.

*****

The group rode the rest of the way in silence. The only sounds heard were the soft snores of Andrew and Ayanna humming to Row, Row, Row Your Boat. When they finally arrived back at the house, Ayanna continued to sing louder and louder.

"Yani, please cut out all that noise girl. I'm tired. Why don't you go to the den and play with your Simon Says." Lynette said wearily.

"Mama, I wanna color."

Lynette was so tired she could hardly see straight. The daily chores, working all night, getting up early and working a morning job, taking care of her child, and she still had to deal with her father's antics; it was all beginning to take a toll on her.

"That's fine Yani. Go get your coloring books and you can color in the den while I hang up the rest of these clothes on the line and cook supper."

While Ayanna jumped out of the car and was bouncing up to the back door, Lynette and Rita managed to get Andrew out of the car and half-walked, half dragged him into the house and laid him in his bed. He promptly snorted and rolled over to his side.

Rita turned to Lynette. "Well Netty, it's time for me to get out of here. I've got some shopping to do before Clarence gets home."

Lynette narrowed her eyes and stared Rita down who promptly looked away.

"I don't know why you're still messing with his sorry ass. He doesn't work and all he does is run the damn streets."

Rita rolled her eyes but inched towards the door for an escape.

"Don't be telling me nothing about my man. He treats

me good and plus he's fine." Rita said half-heartedly but still managed to roll her neck.

Lynette didn't have the heart to tell her that, no, her man was not fine. In fact, at five feet seven inches, one-hundred and twenty pounds soaking wet, and sporting a Geri Curl that he constantly sprayed to keep wet; he looked like a crack-head Jermaine Jackson.

"Okay Rita. If you say so. All I know is Clarence is lazy and sorry as hell. You know you can do better."

Instead of trying to defend Clarence again, Rita inched toward the back door some more. As she was leaving, she spotted a red pick-up truck pulling up in the yard.

"Netty, here comes Jerome. I'm going to get out of here because I don't want to hear ya'll arguing again.

"I don't start anything. He does. I'm tired of him walking around here like he's a damn king or something."

Rita wasn't buying it. "It doesn't matter who starts it. He's mean as a snake like your daddy and you're stubborn as a mule like your mama. God rest her soul."

Lynette blinked back tears at the mention of her mother and was ready for Rita to take her behind home.

"Rita, I'll see you tomorrow girl. Thanks for helping me find Ayanna and my daddy."

"No problem. You know I'll do anything for li'l Netty. She's my favorite godchild."

Lynette giggled. "She's your only godchild. Now go on home to your man."

Rita gave her an evil look and walked out the door. "Bye girl." She greeted Jerome as he came up the steps.

"Hey Jerome."

"Hey Rita. How ya doing today?" Jerome greeted her with a smile a mile wide. Lynette wanted to throw up.

"I'm doing fine. I'll see you two later." Rita walked back down the gravel driveway to her house.

As soon as Rita was out of sight, the smile dropped from Jerome's face. He stared at Lynette and brushed past her without saying a word.

"You could at least speak. You don't see me standing here?" Lynette stood taller and ready to do battle if needed.

Instead of responding, Jerome just kept walking in silence. He then went to his room in the back of the house and slammed the door.

Lynette was used to her brother's attitude. Ever since their mother had died, Jerome would snap unexpectedly and preferred to be alone. He did landscaping work independently and rebuilt engines for cars on the side. One would think that Jerome being a landscaper would mean that the land and house would be beautiful, but there was nothing other than broken down cars, making the place look like a junkyard.

Lynette loved her brother dearly and she longed to have the old Jerome back who was happy and mischievous. But right now, she couldn't worry about the past. She had too much on her plate at the present time. Lynette shook her head and went outside to hang the rest of the clothes on the line and finish her chores for the day.

*****

Lynette woke up to the sounds of moaning. At first, disoriented, she didn't know where she was or what time it was. She looked over at the clock on the nightstand. It read 2:13am. Then she heard it again. There was a faint moaning sound outside of her door. She quickly put on her robe and opened her door to step out of the room. On stepping into the hall, she nearly tripped over her father. He was crouched down by her bedroom door rocking back and forth. When he saw Lynette staring down at him frozen in shock, he smiled at her with an almost child-like grin.

"Guess what baby girl? Your mama came to see me."

Lynette just continued to stare at her father and remained silent. She had gone through these routine countless times since her mom's passing a few years back but never in the early hours of the morning. It usually happened after a day of heavy drinking and a visit to her mother's grave.

Meanwhile, Andrew continued to ramble on.

"She said that the annual fish fry is coming up and she needs me and the fellas to whip up a batch of lightning." He then got misty-eyed. "That woman always did know how to throw a damn good party. We'll have the best food and liquor this side of the James River".

"Don't forget the Bridge games that mama always runs, daddy." Lynette stated. It was best to let this conversation run its course.

"That's right baby girl. Your mama can beat the drawers off any of those fools." He was obviously pleased about his deceased wife's uncanny ability to whip anybody at a game of cards.

Lynette closed her eyes and prayed for strength. She managed to help her father off the floor while he was still rambling about his deceased wife. She then helped Andrew to his bed. He gingerly got under the covers with a smile on his face and whispered, "See. Your mama is here right now." He then closed his eyes and went to sleep.

Lynette thought that her father was truly losing his mind. He was always saying that her mother was with them physically. She wouldn't be as worried if he was referring to her mother's spirit. Lynette knew that he was just grieving but she wondered if he would ever get better.

Then, suddenly, his face changed and contorted into something that resembled pain. "No son! I've had enough! The old man can't take no more!" Andrew's arm had flown up to his face protecting it from some unseen force. He whimpered and rocked from side to side.

Lynette knew instantly what that force was that was causing her father so much pain. She had seen it firsthand. "Poor daddy. You're seeing things that aren't there. I wish I could make your pain go away. I wish I could protect you better."

Lynette then quietly went back to her room thinking about who would take her pain away.

Back in her bed, Lynette couldn't go back to sleep. The sounds of her father's whimpering echoing in her mind kept her wide awake. She knew that her father was feeling pain from Jerome's blows; blows that he usually kept to the body so people wouldn't see them. She herself had sustained some of those body blows while attempting to protect her father from her brother's wrath. Jerome usually abused Andrew while he was drunk; afraid of what his father might do if he was sober. Most of the time it was verbal abuse or shoving, but there were occasions when Jerome went too far. Lynette could remember coming home from the grocery store almost a year ago. Rita had been watching Ayanna while she was at work.

As she pulled up in the yard, Lynette could remember the look of fear and anguish on Rita's face as she ran up to her car.

"Netty! Oh my Lord, Netty! You got to help your daddy!" Rita was practically hanging from the window that Lynette had rolled down.

"Rita, get off the window before you trip and fall and what's going on with my daddy?" Lynette parked her car beside the weeping willow and jumped out, groceries completely forgotten.

Rita was shaking from head to toe and pointing to the woods behind the tool shed. "Jerome got mad at daddy for feeding his dogs and he dragged him down to the woods. I never seen him so mad, Netty. I could hear your daddy yelling just before you came home." Tears were streaming down Rita's face.

Lynette told Rita to hurry to the house and get Ayanna and take her back to her house across the street. Lynette would come and get her in a little while.

She was tired of her brother and the way he disrespected their father. She grabbed her baseball bat from the floor behind the driver's seat. She kept it there for protection and would have no problem using it at that moment for her father's protection.

"I'm sick of this shit! I mean it!" Lynette yelled aloud as she turned three shades of red and started shaking. "God please give me strength."

She glanced towards the house to make sure that Ayanna had made it inside and then ran off towards the woods. She was determined to get to her father before Jerome inflicted any permanent damage on him. How could a son be so cruel and unloving? Lynette couldn't fathom hurting her father. She loved him despite all his shortcomings and he didn't deserve to be treated like this. There was no use telling her other brothers and sisters because they would just issue idle threats and do nothing about it. Lynette had gone to them once before and none of them believed her; that, or they just didn't want to get involved. Cowards. At that moment, Lynette despised them all because here she was again, the baby girl, on her own to protect her father.

All of a sudden, she heard dull thuds coming from a short distance. She ran quietly towards the sounds and screamed when she saw what Jerome was doing. On the ground next to a tree, was Andrew with a bloody lip and his head was hunched over. Jerome was standing to the side and beating him with a thick leather belt with a look of pure evil triumph. It sent chills up Lynette's spine. Jerome stopped and turned toward the sound of his sister's scream. His triumphant look turned to shock when he realized she had witnessed what he had been doing. But, suddenly, his face went blank and he shrugged his shoulders.

"So now you know." He smirked at Lynette and looked down at the bat in her hands. "What are you going to do?"

Lynette had completely forgotten about the bat when she had witnessed her brother beating Andrew. He was moaning softly, still slumped against the tree. Suddenly she snapped out of her trance.

"What am I going do?" She spat. "Nigga!"

She swung the bat with such lightning speed and accuracy, Jerome didn't have a chance dodge attack. The bat caught him in the ribs and he went down to his knees.

"You a crazy bitch!" He choked out as he clutched his side.

"You out here beating up on your daddy and I'm crazy?" She drew the bat back and hit him again; this time in the shoulder. "You should be ashamed of yourself" She screamed as she watched him lying on the ground rocking back and forth, while holding his ribs and shoulder. "You ain't putting your hands on my daddy no more. I'm making sure of that this time."

While Jerome was still on the ground, Lynette managed to help up a very weak Andrew and they walked slowly back to the house. They could hear Jerome cursing them as they got further and further away. Later the police came but Andrew blamed his bruises on clumsiness and refused to press charges on Jerome, to Lynette's dismay. Lynette said everything she could to convince him to press charges and send Jerome to jail but Andrew refused. Jerome had won once again.

Lynette sighed and rolled over to her side. She had called her sisters and told them what happened. They had been angry and came to talk to Andrew but he denied it all, saying that he didn't know what Lynette was talking about. In the end, they had just issued empty threats to Jerome, who swore he didn't touch their father, and dropped the matter altogether. This hadn't been unexpected by Lynette but she was still hurt deeply. She was the only person there for him, and, as always, he had turned his back on her and made her look foolish. One day he wouldn't have her and Lynette took comfort in knowing that her family would get a taste of their own medicine.

Second Chapter

It was Saturday night and Lynette was ready to unwind. She had been out all day, shopping with her sisters – Lynda, Catheryn, and Simone. Lynette loved shopping with her sisters but they were masters at making a full day out of any shopping experience. All Lynette wanted to do was soak her feet in a tub of warm water and Epsom Salt. She was about to run a hot bath when the phone rang. She ran into the den to pick up the phone and at the same time her brother, Jerome, picked it up from the living room.

"Hello?" Lynette answered.

"Hello!" Jerome answered impatiently.

"M-m-m-may I speak to Lynette?" A flustered male voice responded.

"I've got it Jerome. You can hang up now."

Lynette couldn't quite make out everything her brother muttered as he hung up but she caught ".....different niggas."

There were a few seconds of uncomfortable silence before Lynette spoke up.

"Who is this?"

"It's me, Michael, li'l mama. Whatcha getting into tonight?"

Lynette grinned from ear to ear. They had known

each other since high school. Michael was a 6ft 2in, deep chocolate, well chiseled man. He had a smile that could melt any woman's heart along with a slick charismatic nature that had women literally throwing themselves in his bed. Michael had tried on numerous occasions to bed Lynette but she wasn't falling for it. She knew his track record with women. They had remained friends for six years now.

"I'm about to run me some bath water. I've been out all day with my sisters shopping and my dogs are tired. You know how they are when they get together."

"Damn. You were with all three of them? They will make a nigga pass out."

"Tell me about it" Lynette was thinking about putting a few drops of Jasmine oil in her bath water. She loved how soft it made her skin feel and how the musky scent made her smell. She was ready for Michael to say why he called.

As if reading her mind, Michael got right to the point. "Well, lil mama, we're havin a party over on Twenty-Fifth Street and I was calling to see if you wanted me to come and pick you up. Bobby already got the music, drinks, and smoke. We just trying to get up with the people."

There was a quick intake of breath and then a slow exhale. "We already getting this party started", as he coughed once.

Lynette couldn't help but laugh at Michael. He could easily out-smoke any Rasta. She could use some good smoke and a good laugh and Michael could provide both.

"Yeah. I don't mind you picking me up but I don't want Ayanna with my daddy tonight". Lynette had smelled liquor on Andrew's breath when she had come in earlier from shopping.

Another exhale. "Don't worry about that lil mama. She

can hang out with Precious upstairs. You know how they like to play together." Precious was Michael's five-year-old daughter that he had full custody of. Precious's mother had been in and out of jail for prostitution and drug dealing. Her latest escapade had cost her five years in prison on a plea bargain, after selling cocaine to an undercover narcotics agent. Michael had quickly stepped in and obtained complete parental rights and vowed never to let Precious to go back to her mother. It was just one of the many traits that Lynette loved about him.

"Alright. Just let me take a quick bath and put some clothes on Ayanna. How about you give me an hour. Cool?"

"That's cool lil mama. I need to call some mo' people and help Bobby finish setting up anyway. See you in an hour."

Lynette hung up the phone still grinning. She hurried to the bathroom to take a bath. Afterwards, she put a cute hot-pink overall jumper with purple flowers on the pockets on Ayanna. Lynette stepped back to admire her precious daughter. She was short for a five-year-old. But Lynette knew she would be tall because her feet were two sizes too big for her. She had bright eyes and a smooth caramel complexion. The only problem was her mouth. It was so big a deaf man could hear her. Lynette was constantly getting on her for talking so much. Tonight was no different.

"Mama, where we goin?"

"You'll see when we get there. It's a surprise. I've told you about asking so many questions."

"Mama you look pretty." Ayanna said trying to change the subject. Lynette shook her head. The child was too smart for her own good.

"Thank you. So do you." Lynette had opted to wear

beige hot-pants and a multicolored baby-doll shirt. Lynette was trying to buckle Ayanna's shoes but she kept squirming around. The child could never keep still.

"Ayanna, keep still before I pop you. We've got to get ready to leave soon." Ayanna instantly stopped squirming knowing that her mother wasn't playing.

"Mama, we're gonna have some fun? I wanna stay up late!" Ayanna was grinning from ear to ear in anticipation of staying up with the adults.

Lynette quickly glanced at her clock on the night-stand. They only had ten minutes to get ready and Michael was always on time.

"Yes baby. We're going to have some fun. You and Precious get to play together and stay up until Mama gets tired." Lynette tickled her daughter who squealed. "And Mama can stay up all night long!"

That did it. Ayanna jumped up and ran to the door ready to go. "Come on Mama. Let's go! Let's go!"

"Chile, you better hold up. Mama's not driving. Uncle Mike is picking us up."

As if on cue, bright headlights flooded the kitchen window and Marvin Gaye's Sexual Healing could be heard from Michael's 75 Impala.

"Who' playing that damn music?" Andrew had been in his room sleeping until the music woke him up.

"It's nobody daddy. Me and Ayanna are gone. Bye!" Lynette hurried her daughter out to the car. "Turn that down Michael. I already got to hear my dad's mouth on a regular basis. Damn."

"My bad lil mama." Michael turned down the music. "Hey lil Netty." He pinched Ayanna's cheeks. "I swear this girl got your spunk Netty. She going to be a heartbreaker too like her mama."

Ayanna started giggling. "Hi Uncle Mike. What's that?" Ayanna was pointing to the Cheech and Chong sized joint burning in Michael's ashtray.

Lynette glared at Michael.

"Oh, that's just incense to make the car smell good, lil Netty." He glanced nervously over at Lynette. "It smells good enough now so let me put that out." He quickly put out the enormous joint and closed the ashtray.

"Let's go have some fun mama."

Lynette smiled at her daughter. "Yeah baby. We're going to have some fun tonight."

*****

"This party is jumpin!"

Lynette had to agree with Michael. They were listening to Rock with You from Michael Jackson's Off The Wall album. There were people dancing and laughing on the dance floor in the middle of the massive living room. People were sitting on couches, eating fried fish and chicken, while carrying on animated conversations. Various rooms were filled with smoke and others with cards and dice games. From time to time, you would hear some poor loser cursing because they had lost their last five dollars, or someone bragging about their winnings. Lynette had just come from upstairs having checked on Ayanna and Precious. They had been inseparable since they were born and were as close as sisters could be. When she left them, they had been arguing over who was going to be in charge of pouring the imaginary tea at their tea party. Lynette didn't know how they got along so well. They were both bossy as hell.

Lynette, who had a good buzz, pulled Michael to the dance floor. "Come on and let me show you how to really get down."

Michael knew Lynette was the best on the dance floor but still couldn't resist a challenge.

"You are going to show me how it's done, huh? Come on and put your money where your mouth is."

When they got to the dance floor, however, Michael knew it was over. The way Lynette was dropping to the floor and moving her hips, you would have thought she was a Soul Train dancer.

"Damn, lil mama, slow down. I'm not going to be able to keep up with your ass much longer."

Lynette dropped back down to the floor, came back up and laughed. "You haven't kept up with me since we started. I told you I was going to show you how to get down."

All of a sudden, the hairs on the back of Lynette's neck stood up. She looked over by the front door and saw a heavy-set, short, extremely pale guy standing up against the wall. He had a hood on his head so Lynette couldn't see his features very well. He looked like a ghost among all the shades of brown that were surrounding him. Lynette couldn't place her finger on it but the guy just didn't seem right. A voice was telling her it was time to leave.

"Michael, I've been here long enough. It's getting really late and I want to go ahead and take Ayanna home. You don't mind, do you?" Her voice held a hint of fear.

Michael was disappointed in Lynette's sudden change of mood and was caught a little off guard.

"Damn. You got to leave now? We were just starting to get our groove on."

"I know Mike but I don't want to have Ayanna out too late."

"Well, hell, it's already past twelve. You might as well let her stay up a little bit longer. Leave the girls alone. They having fun up there doing their little cute party shit." Michael gave a smile that usually made women hearts melt. But Lynette knew Michael too well. She gave him an evil look and he threw up his hands and sighed. He started to walk away but sensed there was something Lynette wasn't telling him. "What's going on Netty? We were just dancing and having a good time a minute ago and now you're acting like you just saw a ghost." He said not knowing just how true that statement was.

Lynette's eyes darted to the front door before focusing back on her friend. "I saw someone who didn't look like he belonged here and I'm trying to get the hell outta dodge. That's what's going on."

"Netty, you're being paranoid."

"Mike...."

"Netty come on now..." Michael continued to try and plead.

"Michael, I said I want to go home!" Lynette's buzz was completely gone.

Michael didn't want Lynette to go but he knew there was nothing he could say to change her mind. "Alright. Stay right here and let me put Precious to bed really quick and get Ayanna."

Lynette was still feeling uneasy and didn't trust Precious at the party without her father there. "No, get Precious too.

She might get nosey or scared and come downstairs looking for you. I'm feeling real uneasy."

Michael shook his head. "She'll be okay. You were right. The kids don't need to be up no later. She knows not to come downstairs and ain't nobody stupid enough to put their hands on her. Plus, I got Bobby. You know he's like my brother. He definitely not gonna let nothing happen to her."

"But… …."

"Damn, Netty! I said she's going to be fine. These are my people. I'll let Bobby know before we go."

Lynette threw her hands up and surrendered. "My bad Mike. You're right."

Michael felt guilty about snapping at Lynette. "It's cool ma. Let me get lil Netty and put Precious to bed."

As soon as Michael left to go upstairs, Lynette glanced over at the front door again. The strange pale guy was gone. She searched the crowd but couldn't see him. She still felt uneasy for some reason.

Michael came downstairs a few moments later carrying a sleeping Ayanna. "Those two were already passed out in their teacups." Michael chuckled.

Lynette reached for her daughter. "There's my baby. Are you tired?"

Even though Ayanna's head was leaning to the side, she quickly replied, "No, I'm not sleepy mama." Then her head drooped back down to her shoulder.

Lynette couldn't help but look at Michael and giggle. The trio quickly made it to Michael's Impala and were about ten minutes into to drive when Michael cursed under his breath and started turning the car back around to go back to his house.

Lynette, who had been nodding off, quickly sat up straight. "What are you doing?"

"I forgot my wallet. You live out in the damn woods so I'm going to have to stop and get some gas on the way back. As a matter of fact, I'm going to need some papers too. We ain't gone that far from the house yet so I'm going to turn back really quick."

Lynette smacked her lips and laid her head back on the seat. When they were about a block away from Michael's house, they could hear gunshots.

"Oh shit! Somebody's blastin! Both of you get down!" Michael reached down under the seat to get his 9mm pistol.

"Ayanna, put your head down baby!" Lynette quickly reached out to the backseat and pulled a frightened Ayanna down to the floor.

"Shit. I can't tell where the shots are coming from." Michael had put the gun in his lap ready for whatever was going to happen.

But, as they inched a little closer to Michael's house, they saw figures running from the house wearing hoods. They quickly jumped in a car parked on the corner and sped away with the tires screeching.

Michael stopped the car and jumped out with his gun in his hand. "What the.....? I know them niggas didn't just run out of my house?" Then the realization that Precious was in the house hit him like a ton of bricks. "Oh shit! Precious!" Michael took off inside.

Everyone had come out of their homes after the shots stopped firing to see what had happened. Lynette spotted Ayanna's old baby-sitter, Mrs. Winston who lived across the street. She grabbed Ayanna and quickly ran to the old woman.

"Mrs. Winston, could you watch Yani for me while I go with Michael inside?"

The frail mocha colored old woman smiled at Lynette and then looked across the street and her smiled dropped.

"This used to be a good neighborhood. It's a shame how these thugs taking over." She looked back at Lynette with worry in her bluing eyes. "Of course, I'll watch her, baby."

Lynette thanked her and made a mad dash back across the street and up the steps into Michael's house. What greeted her was pure disaster. There was blood on the walls and bullet holes everywhere. Broken overturned furniture littered the floor from people trying to escape the mayhem. There were people lying in all kind of positions stretched out on sofas, the floor, and the tables. There were visibly shaken people huddled in corners in various rooms as Lynette made her way through the house looking for Michael. Tears welled up in her eyes when she spotted Bobby among the deceased. Lynette almost threw up several times but she knew she had to keep it together. She ran up the stairs in search of Michael and Precious. Again, she went from room to room until a soft moaning stopped her in her tracks. She headed to the bathroom and gasped when she opened the door. She gripped the inside of the doorway to steady herself. Michael was on the floor covered in blood cradling a lifeless Precious. It appeared that she had been shot in the chest. Michael looked up at Lynette with pain-filled eyes before closing them and letting out the most heart-wrenching wail that Lynette could ever imagine. She dropped to her knees beside him.

"I'm so sorry. I'm so sorry," Lynette choked out.

"I found her at the top of the stairs. She must have come out of her room when she heard all the commotion." Michael clinched his fists. "I'm going to kill those muthafuckas," Michael whispered with anger and conviction that Lynette had never heard from him before.

"They're going to pay for taking my baby away from me."

Lynette could only nod her head because she knew he would carry out his threat.

Thank you, Jesus, for getting us out of here on time. If only I could have convinced Michael to listen to me... Precious would still be alive and I know that the guilt is eating him up... like it's eating me up. Maybe it was her time to go, but, I don't understand. I only ask that you give her father the strength to carry on. I know that Precious is safe in your arms now.

Lynette then put her arms around Michael and they cried together until there were no more tears left.

*****

The funeral for Precious was held at Johnson's Funeral Home in the Churchill area a week later. Not only were the family members there but there were also several news stations there reporting on the tragedy. Many supporters, both black and white, also showed up to offer their condolences. People were outraged at the violence which had claimed so many lives, and had held a candle-lit gathering the night before for those slain. Because Precious was so young, locals were even more saddened and angered and Michael had taken some backlash for leaving her that night. This had only added to his despair. Michael had Precious in a beautiful white coffin with pink roses lining the outside and a white silk lining on the inside. Precious looked like a young Sleeping Beauty with her hair in Shirley Temple curls and a white dress with ruffles on the bottom.

Lynette was sitting on the front pew beside Michael holding his hand. He was staring straight ahead as if in a trance. Lynette squeezed his hand for reassurance.

"We'll get through this together," she whispered.

He squeezed her hand back.

Ayanna, who was sitting with one of Michael's cousins, had taken Precious's death very well. The night after the shooting, she had asked her mother if she could give her favorite doll away to some friend who needed it. At first, Lynette said no until Ayanna explained that Precious was the friend and didn't have anything to play with in heaven. After all, Jesus said it was better to give than to receive, she had told her mother. Ayanna now quietly held the doll in her arms.

The pastor gave a beautiful eulogy and later on, when the pastor finished his prayer by the gravesite, Ayanna lay her favorite doll on the coffin.

"Now she won't be alone Uncle Mike." Ayanna gazed at Michael with a smile and grabbed his hand.

Michael couldn't hold it any longer and broke down weeping.

"Come on Michael. It's going to be alright." Lynette grabbed him tightly. "It's going to be alright. Let's get back to your mama's place and you can get yourself together."

Michael looked at Lynette through teary eyes. "Thank you for being here Netty. I don't know what I'd do if you weren't here with me."

Lynette released him and looked up into his swollen eyes. "You are my family, Mike. Of course, I'm here for you. I wouldn't have it any other way."

Michael picked Ayanna up and together they walked back to the awaiting limo.

*****

"I'm so ready for this day to be over."

Lynette was in Michael's mother's sitting room observing the elderly women gossiping. Mrs. Winston was among the gossiping group but looked as if she would rather be somewhere else. She spotted Lynette across the room and quickly excused herself from the women. She slowly walked over to Lynette and placed a gentle hand on her shoulder.

"How are you doing child?" Mrs. Winston barely whispered.

Lynette turned her head, not wanting Mrs. Winston to see the new tears that had sprang up. "I just can't believe that she's gone."

Mrs. Winston patted Lynette's shoulder. "She's with the Father now child. Only He knows why He brought her home so soon and it's not for us to try and figure out why. We just honor her memory." She smiled and looked off into space just simply remembering the rambunctious little girl.

"I'll try Mrs. Winston but it's going to be hard. Ayanna and I will get through this." She paused. "But I don't know about Michael."

Lynette was extremely worried about Michael. He had locked himself in his old room and was refusing to see anyone; even Lynette. She knew that Michael was supposed to mourn but the way he looked at her while holding her (his lifeless daughter), and the way he said he would kill Precious's murderers sent chills up her spine. He wasn't stable so Lynette had to do everything she could to protect him.

Mrs. Winston's soft voice brought her back from her thoughts. "… …..and prayer is all that young man needs child."

"You're so right, Mrs. Winston. Thank you."

Lynette decided that she would try to talk to Michael one last time and then grab Ayanna and head home. She gave her old babysitter a reassuring smile and headed upstairs. She quietly knocked on Michael's old bedroom door. No answer.

Lynette tapped lightly. "Michael, it's me." Still no answer.

She turned the knob but the door wouldn't budge. "Come on Michael and let me in. You know I just want to be here for you. Please, don't shut me out like this."

After a few moments of silence, Lynette heard the lock click. She took a deep breath and pushed the door open. As she stepped in, she wished she would have held her breath a little longer. The room smelled of stale whiskey and Michael was a mess. His eyes were bloodshot, his tie was hanging loosely around his neck, and his suit looked like he had slept in it all night. Lynette decided to be cautious and took baby steps toward him.

"Michael… …?"

"What bastard would do that to a little girl, Netty?" He looked like a neglected child crumpled on the edge of his old bed.

"I don't know, Mike. Some people are heartless and just don't care."

Michael's face suddenly turned vicious. "I just wish I knew who did it!"

Lynette stared at him for a few moments and thought back to that night.

"Remember I told you I saw a strange looking guy at the

party. He just didn't seem right. He looked like a white guy but I know he was a brotha."

Michael looked at Lynette like a deer in headlights.

"You said he looked like a white boy?"

"Yeah, but he had the nose and lips like a brotha."

"Was he short?"

"Yeah. He looked a little on the short side?"

"Did he have a dirty-brown 'fro?"

"I don't know Mike. I couldn't tell. He had a hood on." Lynette was wondering where this line of questioning was going.

Michael suddenly stood up and kicked over the nightstand. The lamp and the drawers came crashing to the floor.

Lynette jumped back. "Michael, what are you doing?"

Suddenly there was a knock on the door. "Is everything alright in there?" It was Michael's mother.

"Yes. Everything is okay." Lynette replied.

"Oh. Okay then." Michael's mother answered hesitantly.

Lynette waited until she heard footsteps retreating before she turned back to Michael.

"Now what's going on?"

Michael stood in front of Lynette and was so close she could smell the Jack Daniel's on his breath.

"I really wish you would have told me this sooner, Netty," he paused. "It was Ghost Face."

Lynette looked dumbfounded. "I tried, Mike, and who is Ghost Face?"

Michael turned away from her. "Everyone calls him Ghost Face because he's an Albino. He's a soldier for Pretty Ricky across the river."

"Southside? You don't even fool with Southside niggas. None of us do. They think they're better than everyone else."

"Yeah, well....I had a run-in with Ricky when I was promoting a party in the West End. He was trying to get a cut and sell some garbage grass in the club but I wasn't having it, so I called him out in front of everybody. That nigga said he was going to get back at me but I didn't think he would come this hard. You don't get at a nigga's seed like that!" He looked at Lynette for what seemed like an eternity to her. "He took my baby and now I'm going to take his life." The look in his eyes as he said this was a blood shot mixture of pure hatred and cold murder.

Later on that night, Lynette received a call from her sister – Catheryn – who sounded frantic.

"Netty, turn on channel twelve!"

"Girl, what is it? I'm about to watch a movie."

"Just turn to the damn news!"

"Damn, okay." Lynette got up and turned to Channel 12. What she saw nearly gave her a heart attack. The news anchor was speaking and a picture of Michael, taken at his daughter's funeral, was in the corner of the screen.

".....and resulted in the deaths of both Shawn 'Pretty Ricky' Evans and Michael Parker. You may all know Parker as the father of five-year-old Precious Parker whose life also tragically ended in gunfire just recently. Police are still investigating the circumstances surrounding Evan's and Parker's deaths but we will keep you informed as the investigation progresses."

Lynette felt like she couldn't catch her breath. Michael was gone? He couldn't be. She could hear someone calling her name in the distance. Could it be him? No, it was too high pitched.

"... ... Lynette. Lynette are you there? Talk to me girl."

But Lynette couldn't speak. She couldn't think. If she had insisted that Precious go with them, if she had just taken Precious no matter what Michael said, maybe they would have been okay. Why hadn't she kept her mouth shut and not revealed who she had seen that night at the party? Michael would be alive right now to make her laugh. She had done everything wrong and as a result had cost both her and her daughter their best friends. She pulled her knees to her chest and cried bitterly.

Third Chapter

"You need to have a talk with your daughter about her daddy, Netty." Simone, Rita, and Lynette were sitting under the weeping willow tree at the back of Andrew's house, discussing while snapping green beans. Simone had made this comment.

She was a thirty-one-year-old single woman with three children. All of them had different fathers; none of them remembered their fathers; and all of them (the children) wished that the next man who came over to talk to their mom would claim the role.

"Simone leave me alone. Eddy does not give a damn about her. She's better off without his sorry ass."

"All I'm saying is that the girl is going to ask questions one day. What then?"

"She's right, Netty," Rita said barely looking up from the beans. "It might come back to haunt you."

Lynette cut her eyes at Rita. "I know what I'm doing. I'll tell her when she's ready. It will be when I think she's ready."

She gave Simone a dirty look for bringing up the subject. "When are you going to find out who Lashay, Nita, and Boo-Boo's daddies are? Or are you still betting on every Tom, Dick, and Tyrone that comes through your door?"

Lynette instantly regretted what she said. When she glimpsed the hurt on her sister's face, she felt even worse.

Even Rita was surprised at Lynette's comment. "Damn, Netty. Was that called for?" She asked.

"I'm sorry, sis. I didn't mean to say that. I just instantly get mad when I think about Eddie." Lynette reached over and patted Simone's hand. "You do take good care of my nieces and nephew." And she meant it.

Simone's eyes brightened a little. "It's alright. I know I could do better when it comes to their daddies. But we're talking about you. You've been lying to her and when she finds out the truth, she's going to blame you. That's all I'm saying."

Lynette gave out a heavy sigh. Deep down within herself, she knew her sisters were right. She just didn't want her daughter to be disappointed. Sure, Ayanna had her grandfather. But it wasn't the same as having her real father. Up until now, Lynette had done everything in her power to shield her from the truth. Maybe, now was the time. She was eleven years old and more curious than ever.

"Both of you are right. I'll give his sister a call and see if she can tell me where that nigga is"

Rita looked up from her green beans and smiled at Lynette. "Good for you girl. You never know, things might turn out alright. Once he sees her, he won't be able to deny her. That's for damn sure."

Lynette grunted. "He did enough of that when I was pregnant with her."

They went on snapping beans and gossiping until it started getting dark and then, Rita and Simone called it a day and went home. Ayanna was spending the night over at her sister - Lynda's house, so Lynette had some time to herself. She thought back to the conversation she had with her sister and best friend. She was still unsure of her decision to let Ayanna meet her father. As she lay across her bed, she could still hear his cold words ringing in her ears.

"You know that ain't my baby, bitch!"

"Who the hell are you calling a bitch, you no class faggot!"

Lynette was standing on the corner in front of the Mosby Court Projects. She had tracked Eddie there, and met him laughing with his friends. She was tired of him not owning up to the fact that she was carrying his child.

Eddie glared down at her. "What you say? Girl, don't make me fuck you up in front of all these nice people." His friends were witnessing the scene, while laughing at Lynette.

"You ain't going to do shit!" Lynette screamed. "My brother, Anthony, owns this spot. You make a move and he'll have the whole projects up your sorry ass!"

Eddie backed down a little. He knew what her crazy oldest brother was capable of. "Girl, what you come up her for? I don't want you no damn more. I moved on and I suggest you do the same."

Lynette folded her arms as best she could above her growing stomach. "I don't want you either. What I want is for you to take care of your baby."

"I'm taking care of my baby. My son. So get out of here with that bullshit and don't come back." Eddie sneered at her.

Lynette heard his friends still snickering behind him at her expense.

Lynette turned out the lights and continued to think of

the few short months she had been with Eddie. Only God knew how she was going to face him without spitting in his arrogant face, but she would face him anyway. She would face her demon after all these years.

For Ayanna.

Yes.

Ayanna would see for herself who he was, and she would turn to her mother for comfort. Soon Ayanna would forget about her father and go on to bigger and better things. Lynette closed her eyes, desperate to get a good night's sleep. But, as more memories flooded her head, sleep was getting farther from her eyes.

Lynette woke up the next morning to the smell of pancakes. She looked over at her clock and it was 6:40am. She tried to drift back to sleep again, but it was too late, she was wide awake. She slipped on her robe and slippers and shuffled her way to the kitchen. She spotted Jerome, who had stayed clear of the house for weeks after the encounter in the woods, looking down at the cast iron pan on the stove with a look of dismay.

"What's wrong with you?" Lynette didn't bother with morning pleasantries.

"These pancakes don't look right." He said without bothering to look up.

Lynette went closer to look in the pan. It infuriated her that she still loved him so much still. When she looked down, all she saw was a light brown watery substance in the shape of the pan.

"How much water or milk did you put in the mix, Jerome. Damn! You can't eat this. Just sit down. I've got this."

Lynette pushed Jerome out of the way with her elbow. After dumping out her brother's watery concoction and making a new batch of pancake mixture, complete with a dash of cinnamon, she soon had a nice plate of steaming fluffy pancakes on the table.

Jerome didn't bother to thank her. He just started piling pancakes on his plate.

Lynette wasn't about to accept him being ungrateful. "You're welcome! I try to do something nice for you and you can't even say thank you. Next time, I'll let you go ahead and eat that nasty shit."

There was silence. "Thank you, Lynette," he sounded like he was choking on the words.

"What?" Lynette asked in disbelief.

"You heard me. You know I don't like repeating myself." Jerome said in a huff and continued eating his sister's homemade pancakes.

Lynette threw her hands up in the air. "Alright. I'll take what I can get."

She spent the rest of the Saturday morning cleaning the house and watering the vegetable garden. She loved walking through the perfectly aligned rows. She, Ayanna, and Andrew had planted corn, tomatoes, cabbage, and carrots. This was all done under Andrew's watchful eye of course. He had taught her everything there was to know about gardening.

After her morning chores, she decided to give Eddie's sister, Diane, a call. She had always liked Diane even though she thought Diane was a little too mouthy. She said whatever was on her mind which often got her in trouble. Lynette grabbed her address book from her nightstand and went to the den to make the call. After the fourth ring, a voice with attitude answered the phone.

"Hello? Who's calling my phone?"

"Is this Diane?" Lynette asked, trying to hold back her own attitude.

"I asked first."

Lynette could picture Diane's neck about to roll out of its socket. "Girl, it's me. Lynette. Ayanna's mom?"

"Well, I'll be damned. What's up, girl? We haven't heard from you and my niece in a minute. I thought you were one of those hos Washington has on the side. He thinks he's slick and I'm stupid but I got his number."

"Girl, you're still with Washington? I thought he went to jail for robbing that liquor store on Broad Street."

"He was set up. You know how that goes." Diane casually dismissed the robbery.

Lynette just shook her head because she didn't know how it went. She hated when women made excuses for their trifling men.

"Okay girl. I called to see if you know where your brother is?"

"Who, Eddie?"

"Yeah, Eddie, girl. Who else?"

"I know who you're talking about. He lives around the corner from Siegel's Grocery Store. He's rents out a room. I don't know why he has that dump. You know he works at the Waste Water Treatment plant still?"

Lynette instantly got mad. "Well I haven't seen the fruits of that labor!"

"I hear you. Here, I'll give you the address. I can't get my hands on his new number right now. But, I do want to see my niece. I know she's big now. I should cuss your ass out for keeping her away so long." Diane said with much attitude.

Lynette decided she would let that last comment slide, this time. "I'll tell you like I tell everybody else. My number hasn't changed in all these years and if you wanted to see her, you could've called or looked it up in the phone book if you couldn't remember it."

Secretly, Lynette was glad that Diane had never bothered to call. Ayanna would've asked too many questions.

"I'm not trying to get into it with you, Lynette. We're too cool with each other for that. You and Ayanna come and see me. I'm at my daddy's house."

Diane gave the address and they said quick goodbyes to each other. Diane could be a pain in the ass but Lynette was happy she had gotten what she wanted. She looked down at the piece of paper with Eddie's address on it. She stared at it for what seemed like hours. Should she really go over to his place? Is it really wise? What would she say? Maybe, this was a bad idea. Lynette shook her head trying to clear it. Of course, she should confront him, she decided. Didn't Diane just say he was still working at the waste management plant? He was living carefree and here she was working two jobs to take care of her and Ayanna. Didn't they deserve better? Damn right.

Lynette grabbed her keys off the dining room table and did a quick sweep of her surroundings. Everything was in order, so she didn't have to hear any complaints when she returned. She dashed out the back door, finally ready to confront the father of her child, after so many years.

Fourth Chapter

"Is this it? No, it couldn't be."

Lynette had turned down a gravel alley. She could hear the crunching rocks and prayed she didn't run over any glass. She definitely didn't want to be stranded here. Here actually used to be a run-down row of houses which, in their youth, were beautifully kept by upper-class white people. Now some were occupied by homeless people, their old bordered-up and rat-infested rooms still giving refuge to the needy.

Lynette looked at the address again. Yep. This was the address that Diane had given her. She couldn't believe that Eddie would live like this. He had always prided himself on having the best of everything. She felt a sense of pity, but at the same time she couldn't help but think that it served him right for denying his daughter.

She parked her Mustang by the fence and made sure she locked all the doors and the windows were rolled up. "Of course, that probably wouldn't stop no damn body." Lynette thought to herself.

She walked up to the door and knocked lightly. After a few minutes and no answer, she knocked again with more force. Still no answer. "Damn this." Lynette headed back to the car. After a few steps away from the door, she heard the knob turn and the door opened.

"Who's that?" The voice sounded hoarse but Lynette knew who it belonged to without a doubt.

She slowly turned around and looked in Eddie's eyes. "It's me Eddie. Lynette." The words came out harsher than she had expected.

Eddie jumped back as if someone had shocked him. "Baby Netty?" Lynette cringed. "Damn! I mean I'm saying... ... I wasn't expecting no visit from you. What are you doing here?"

Lynette took slow deep breaths. She wanted to scream at him and tell him he was a worthless bastard. She wanted to tell him how smart Ayanna was that she could outrun any boy in her sixth-grade class. He had missed out on all of the awards Ayanna had received and her birthdays; he had missed out on everything. And she hated him for it.

"I came to talk to you about our daughter."

Eddie instantly became nervous and it showed all over his face.

"Yeah nigga you need to be nervous. You haven't so much as bought her a pack of chewing gum since she was born."

They stood staring at each other for what seemed like an eternity. Finally, Eddie spoke up.

"I'm sorry, Baby Netty I....."

All of a sudden, Eddie's head snapped so quickly to the side that he thought his neck might be sprained. His left cheek was burning with so much intensity, it felt like it was on fire. "What the hell is wrong with you woman? Are you crazy? Don't you put your hands on me no damn more!"

"I told you once before not to call me Baby Netty!" Lynette's chest was heaving up and down from anger and her hand hurt from slapping the hell out of Eddie. "And I don't want to hear no I'm sorry! If you were sorry then you would have done something for Ayanna all these years." She looked Eddie up and down. "Yeah, you sorry alright." Giving the term a whole new meaning.

Eddie threw up his hands. "Okay, Lynette, you win alright? Come on in so we can talk like we got some sense."

Lynette hesitated for a moment before she slowly walked through his front door and being careful not to touch any part of Eddie. She stared at the densely furnished dark room. There was a small kitchenette and a door leading to the bathroom and bedroom. There was pullout sofa, a wooden table with three chairs around it by the window, and a small television against the wall by the sofa resting on a crate. Lynette couldn't believe how low Eddie had sunken.

"If you're still working at the plant, why the hell are you living in this dump? This isn't you, I'm sorry." Lynette was not one to mince words.

"Damn. Why you got to insult my place like that. I just fell on some hard times." He pointed to one of the chairs. "Have a seat."

Lynette preferred to stand but she eased down on the seat anyway. "Look, I don't want to be over here any longer than I have to. I just felt that it was time to talk to you about Ayanna. Everybody has been telling me that I need to tell her the truth about you but I've been too busy protecting her. It's now time for you to step up to the plate." She looked around the room and then really looked at Eddie for the first time. "Hell, it looks like you need to step up to a plate period. Where's all your weight gone?"

Back when they were dating, Eddie had a nice build with

a pair of sexy legs that Lynette had rarely seen on a man. Now he could pass for a stick figure with sunken cheeks and dark circles around his eyes.

Eddie instantly became defensive, naturally, because it was true and he knew that he had fallen off the wagon. "You just keep on throwing shit at me. I told you that I fell on hard times. Damn. I'm barely holding on. I haven't come around because I don't want Ayanna to see me like this." He hung his head, unable to look in Lynette's cold eyes any longer. "She's better off without me, anyway."

As expected, Lynette wasn't buying it. "Nigga, you didn't come around when you did have a decent pot to piss in and a window to throw it out of, so don't give me that shit. You were a coward when you found out I was pregnant, and you denied it with a straight face knowing fully well I was with no one else. You were a coward when she was born, and even when your own mama said she knew that Ayanna was her grandchild, you refused to come around. And you're a coward now for not being man enough to face an eleven-year-old, letting her know where you've been all her life." Lynette was practically spitting at him. She hated Eddie with a passion.

Eddie could do nothing but stare down at the floor. She had broken him down like a drill sergeant does a new recruit. No one had ever talked to him like that. His mother up-held him in everything that he did until Ayanna was born. His mother had called him up that night after visiting hours. She had said that it looked like he had spit Ayanna out. No amount of coaxing could make him go to see his daughter. Going there made him wrong all those months. Going would make him have to face reality and apologize for his past behavior; neither of which he had been willing to do. He had thought often of the two women he had abandoned, and with each passing year grew more and more into depression and drugs. He would ask his sister, Diane, from time to time in an offhanded way if she had heard from Lynette, but it was always the same answer, "Not since Ayanna was a baby," as she would smack her lips. "I don't know why she thinks she's too good to come around us." Eddie wished he could take it all back but what was done was done. He couldn't change it. But, he would get his act together.

"Look Baby N....I mean, I'm sor...." His cheek was still warm. "I mean, I'm going to get my shit together. They've been cutting hours at the plant but I got this hustle I'm getting together. Don't look at me like that." He said when he saw the smirk that came across Lynette's face. "It ain't nothing that'll send me to the joint."

Lynette still didn't believe him. "Well what is it, Eddie? We all know how you like fast money."

"It's nothing." Eddie said a little too quickly.

"Nothing huh?" Lynette raised a skeptical eyebrow.

"Yeah, you don't need to know the details. Just know that it'll get a nigga on his feet again. I'm going to do right by both my kids. Sheila won't even let me see Cedric no more. Can you believe that shit?

"Does he really want me to answer that question?" Lynette thought. Instead she changed the subject back to her daughter. "Look. I hear what you're saying, but excuses don't make up for eleven years of not seeing or doing right by your daughter. Who do you think has been feeding her, clothing her, nourishing her, and helping to guide her all of these years? Me. I chose to give birth to her and take responsibility because it wasn't her fault that I conceived her with you. You think it's been easy? Far from it. So, save your woe is me 'cause I've got a few of my own."

Lynette stood up and grabbed her purse, anxious to leave. "I'm bringing Ayanna over to see you next Saturday. She's smart enough to decide for herself whether or not she wants you in her life. She's strong and she'll be able to see through any lies you try to tell her. I'll be right there throughout because I'll be damned If I let you hurt her. How does three o'clock sound?"

Eddie couldn't believe this was happening. He had been dreading the reality of having to face his daughter one day, and explain why he hadn't been around. Would she forgive him? Only one way to find out. "Yeah, three o'clock is good." He said in a sullen voice.

Lynette looked pleased. She was confident Ayanna would hate him on the spot. This episode would be over soon and her daughter would cling to her like never before. "Good, we'll see you Saturday." And with that she hurried out the door with a smile on her face.

*****

"Come here baby and let me talk to you."

It was Friday night and Lynette had avoided the subject of visiting Eddie all week. She felt guilty partly because she would have to admit lying to her daughter, and also because of having to subject to Ayanna to a man like Eddie. But it was necessary, in case someone in her family let anything slip in the future.

"I'm coming, mama!" Ayanna came running in the kitchen out of breath.

"Girl, I told you about running in this house." Lynette gently chastised.

"Sorry mama. Oooooh, that smells good. What's in the oven?" Ayanna was salivating at the mouth from the smell of Lynette's homemade pound cake.

Lynette smiled at her daughter's sweet tooth which quickly vanished when she remembered who she had inherited that trait from. "It's a pound cake baby. I'll let you make the glaze."

"Alright!" Ayanna squealed.

"Sit down. Mama needs to talk to you about something serious."

Lynette watched her daughter get herself seated at the table and marveled at how gorgeous she was. She had dozens of thick long braids hanging down past her shoulders with clear and white beads at the ends. Her hair was so thick and coarse, you could do just about anything with it. She had a honey colored complexion that deepened into a beautiful reddish brown in the summer. Her sharp facial features and high cheek bones gave away her Indian and Ethiopian ancestry. She was starting to get tall with long strong legs from running and riding her bike. She only hung out with boys because girls were too prissy for her.

Lynette scooted her chair next to Ayanna's. "I wanted to talk to you about your father." She watched for a reaction. There was none. "Remember when I told you that your dad had died?"

"Yes mama." Ayanna answered, not understanding. What was her mother getting to?

"Well.....he didn't exactly die." Lynette couldn't remember her hands ever shaking this badly.

Now, Ayanna was really confused. "What do you mean, mama? He really didn't die? What about the bridge and the rain and the....?"

"I know, baby. I know what I told you. That happened to someone else that cared for you very much, but it didn't happen to your father." Lynette wasn't sure if this had been the right thing to do now. "It's just that I thought the truth would hurt you more."

"What's the truth, mama?"

Lynette shifted uncomfortably in her seat. "Well, the truth is that your father and I didn't get along when I was pregnant with you so he chose to stay away. I just recently looked him up and found out where he lives." She knew she was being vague with her daughter; something that she said she would never do. She hated dancing around subjects when it concerned her Ayanna. God, why didn't she gather the strength to do this years ago, instead of making excuses.

Ayanna was quiet for a moment. "So, Tyrell didn't die? He just didn't want to see me?

Lynette looked away, unable to look Ayanna in the eyes. "Your father's name isn't Tyrell. Tyrell is the man who loved you as his own. He's the one who died on the bridge that night drunk behind the wheel. The man I had you by; his name is Eddie. I'm sure he did want to see you but just didn't know how to go about it, baby." Lynette really didn't know what to say.

Ayanna's eyes filled with tears. Many questions were running through her mind. How could her mother lie about something so important? Didn't her mother know how much she longed for a dad? And was her father having it so bad that he didn't want to find his own daughter? She wiped her eyes and looked defiantly at Lynette. "Then he could have come. If I had a daughter, I would never stay away. Doesn't he know where granddaddy stays?"

"Yes, he does but your granddaddy doesn't allow him here."

"I don't care." Ayanna said with hurt in her voice. "He still should have tried."

Lynette reached over to grab her daughter's hand. "Don't cry, baby. I've done the best I can do to make sure you feel loved and to have the things you need." Lynette paused. "Would you like to tell your father how you feel?"

Ayanna sniffled. "Yes." Then she asked, "What's his name again, mama?"

"Eddie Parker."

Silence.

Lynette squeezed Ayanna's hand. "Are you mad at me?"

Ayanna smiled up at her mother. Not a real smile. It was the smile she gave her mother when she was unhappy or angry so Lynette wouldn't worry about her; wouldn't feel guilty about leaving Ayanna to face the world alone with her strong will as an iron shield sometimes. "No ma. I'm not mad at you. When can I see him?"

"Well, how does tomorrow sound?" Lynette still wasn't so sure that Ayanna was up to seeing Eddie on such short notice. But Ayanna seemed to be taking the news better than expected.

"Okay. Can I help you with the glaze now?" Ayanna quickly changed the subject.

Lynette couldn't believe how well it had gone. For a moment, it was touch and go, but Ayanna had bounced back as usual. Lynette always wished that she had her daughter's strength, but couldn't seem to find it. She leaned on Ayanna every day for support while the child ran around oblivious to her mother's pain.

The sweet smells of the pound cake had filled the kitchen, waiting to be glazed.

"Of course, you can help me with the glaze. Hand me the powdered sugar from the pantry and let's get to work."

*****

"I can't believe that my dad's alive!" Ayanna thought as she lay back on her bed later on that night. She didn't want her mother to know that, but yes, she was mad at her. How many times had that monkey-faced Kevin Syler teased her for not having a father and for not having money? He had teased her since the first grade and all the time she had had a father. She could have shown him how smart she was and he would have been too proud of her to stay away. Why didn't her mom try to get in touch with her father sooner? And who was that other person her mom was talking about that had really died? Tomorrow, however, her father would see and he would never go away again. Ayanna was too full of excitement to sleep. "Wait till I tell Kevin and Sheron and Aaron. They won't be laughing anymore."

Lynette could see Ayanna out the corner of her eye bouncing to the music on the radio. The child was too calm, and even though she said she wasn't mad, Lynette sensed her daughter was a little distant towards her that morning. Well, that would change once Ayanna talked to Eddie. They were on their way now to his shabby house.

"You sure you're okay, baby?"

Ayanna kept bobbing her head to the music but looked at her mother. "Yes mama. I'm fine."

Lynette was still a little nervous. "I'm just checking. We can turn back if you want to."

"Oh no, mama. I want to go." Ayanna said quickly. "I have some stuff I want to show him."

Lynette glanced over at Ayanna suspiciously. "What kind of stuff?" She had seen Ayanna rearranging items in her book bag earlier but hadn't questioned it. It now lay at Ayanna's feet.

Ayanna shrugged. "Just some school stuff, ma."

Lynette sighed. "Okay. As long as you don't forget anything over there."

"I won't, mama."

They continued driving for a short while until Lynette spotted the gravel alley leading to their destination. Ayanna couldn't believe that people lived in such rundown houses.

"Mama, do people actually live here?"

"I'm afraid so, baby."

"My dad too?" Ayanna asked with her mouth hanging open and hoping that her mother had the wrong address.

Lynette glanced over at Ayanna. "Yes. Your dad too, unfortunately."

They rode a little further and parked the car. They then walked hand-in-hand up to Eddie's front door. Lynette looked down at Ayanna. "You ready?"

Ayanna just shook her head up and down and squeezed her mother's hand tightly. It felt like she had jumping beans in her stomach.

Lynette knocked on the door and waited. No answer.

"Doesn't he know we're coming, ma?" Ayanna asked nervously.

"Hush up now," Lynette snapped. She could feel herself getting warm. "I know this nigga didn't stand...."

Finally, the door opened and Eddie appeared at the door clean shaven with a wrinkled button down shirt and faded jeans. Ayanna took a step back at the sight of him. Lynette had to admit to herself that he looked a lot better than the last time she saw him. Eddie cleared his throat smiled down at Ayanna. "Hey pretty girl. Do you know who I am?"

Ayanna just stared up at him and didn't say a word.

Lynette decided to intervene. "Ayanna, this is your father, Eddie." Lynette said gently.

"Hi." Was all Ayanna could manage to say. Is this really my dad? Ayanna quickly studied his every facial feature from his hair line to his cheekbones, and then to his chin. She had often stood beside her mother in the mirror and looked for features that matched. She could find none. Now she knew, looking at this man, whose genes had been the strongest. She hated him for it and, not knowing this now, she would deny this fact for the rest of her life. She would never admit to looking like the man who had abandoned her.

Eddie looked like he didn't know which way to turn.

Lynette spoke up again. "Why don't we go inside so you both can get to know each other? Okay?"

Eddie moved aside to let them come inside and said a quick silent prayer that he would be able to get through this ordeal.

After they were situated around the kitchen table, Ayanna opened up. "So why haven't you come around?" Ayanna asked innocently but was straight to the point, nonetheless.

Eddie looked at Lynette for support but received nothing

but silence and a raised eyebrow. He cleared his throat. "Well baby, to be honest, your old man's been stupid."

"Okay, but where have you been?" Ayanna insisted.

Lynette had to suppress a laugh.

Eddie looked extremely flustered at the moment and was struggling for the right words. "Well, like I said, I've been stupid and selfish. I stayed away because I didn't think I would be a good father." He started to reach for her hand but thought better of it. "I'm so sorry I didn't do right by you all this time. I should have been there for you. I haven't had any good luck because of it." Eddie paused and looked at Ayanna with tears in his eyes. "I thought about you all the time. Like how tall you've got to be by now or how smart you are. I know you're smart. You got that from your pop." Eddie smiled nervously.

Lynette spoke up. "She didn't get anything from you but your looks. But trust me, she's a helluva lot better looking. In fact, she's beautiful. This is what you've been missing out on." She didn't care how much DNA her daughter and Eddie shared. She was determined that Ayanna be nothing like him.

Eddie just leaned back in the chair and stared down at the table.

Ayanna wasn't the least bit comfortable and could sense the tension between her parents. There was something about this man that she didn't like. Sure, she had been wanting a dad for a long time, but she wasn't sure that she wanted it to be this homeless looking man sitting across from her. And why did she even think that they would have anything to share together. She had put away any ideas of showing her oratorical and talent show awards to him when he opened up his door. She was nothing like....what's his name? Oh yeah,

Eddie. "Mama, can we go now?" She didn't mean to be rude but she was ready to go home.

"Already?" Lynette couldn't believe Ayanna didn't have more questions. There were tons more that she wanted Ayanna to humiliate Eddie with.

Eddie quickly spoke up. "We've got a lot of catching up to do. You sure you're ready to go?" He was practically pleading with her to stay. Now that he had seen his daughter he wanted to get everything out in the open. Well, almost everything. He wasn't ready to tell her about his drug problems.

Ayanna, however, only addressed her mother. "I'm sure I'm ready to go, ma."

Lynette was jumping for joy inside. This was way easier than she had anticipated. Soon she would be rid of Eddie once and for all without a guilty conscience. "Come on, baby. We don't have to stay if you don't want to."

Eddie jumped up. "Damn! I mean....." He stuttered when he saw the surprised look on Ayanna's face. "We didn't even get a chance to talk. I was hoping that we could spend some time together." He had been building his courage up all week to see his daughter and now this. He had to think of something fast. Meanwhile, Lynette and Ayanna were heading out of the door.

"Well, bye! It was nice to meet you." Ayanna's statement held no truth to it as she waved goodbye.

Lynette gently nudged Ayanna forward. "You go on ahead while I speak to Eddie for a second."

Ayanna looked at Eddie one more time before she turned and headed for the car.

Eddie made one last attempt at keeping Ayanna from

wanting to leave. "Your big brother is going to be disappointed he didn't get to meet you."

Ayanna stopped dead in her tracks. She quickly turned around. "I have a brother?" She couldn't have heard correctly.

Eddie smiled through his anxiety. "Yes, and his name is Cedric."

Lynette sneered at Eddie. "I wasn't ready to tell her about Cedric. Finding out about you was enough for one day. Nigga, you've got some nerve!"

"She has a right to know. Damn, don't be so cold."

While her parents continued to argue, Ayanna was lost in her own thoughts. The news about her having a brother changed everything. She could have him beat up Kevin easily. She wouldn't have to worry about getting teased about having a mom without a husband, a drunk grandfather, and a mean uncle. "All I would have to do would be to sic my big brother on them and those fools would scatter." Ayanna smiled inwardly. Unfortunately, that would mean having to deal with Eddie for a while. "Who knows, he might be alright." She thought. Ayanna looked at her parents who had stopped arguing. Lynette was looking at her with an expression of dismay and Eddie seemed to have a nervous tick and kept wringing his hands. Ayanna still didn't trust him, but she decided to give him a chance. At least, so she could meet her brother. "I want to meet him, mama. Is that okay? Ayanna asked timidly.

Lynette couldn't believe the turn of events, thanks to Eddie and his big mouth. She had been so close to getting rid of him. "Is this really happening?" She thought. "We'll talk about it later, baby." Lynette sighed.

"But mama…"

"I said we'll talk about it later. Go on to the car."

When they were alone, Lynette spoke to Eddie in a low soft voice, but he got the message loud and clear. "If you hurt my daughter, you'll pay. Do you hear me?"

"Look…." Eddie started.

"No! Did you hear me?" Lynette pointed her finger in Eddie's face so close he had to back up. "You'd better know what you're doing and you better have good intentions. I won't let you hurt her like you hurt me. I'll put you in your grave first, nigga." With that, she spun around and followed her daughter.

Fifth Chapter

The next few months were pretty uneventful for Lynette. She was still working her two jobs, but school would soon be ending and she would only be working at Safeway. She would just have to go full-time to make sure she made ends meet. Andrew was his usual self; tending to his garden with occasional nips from his flask tucked away safely in his pants pocket. He also liked to ride his bike to Mr. Carroll's store and sit on the porch, trading old war stories with his longtime friends. Mr. Carroll was a jolly old white man who had always catered to the black community as well as whites. There were several incidents when Andrew and his buddies had to stand up to the Ku Klux Klan outside of Mr. Carroll's store for him for mingling with the colored. Mr. Carroll was appreciative and never segregated his store. He would call Lynette sometimes to get Andrew because he was too tipsy to make it back home. "Your daddy done gone and got himself drunk again. I keep telling him I'm going to throw him off my property one day." Mr. Carroll would chuckle. "But he knows that I don't have the heart to do it."

Jerome was mean as always and never missed a chance to rub Lynette the wrong way. The easiest way to do this was to go after her daughter. Ayanna could have her hair braided up in the cutest styles that her mother would do for her every two weeks. "Look at them beans on the back of your neck. You don't get them from us." Jerome would sneer. Or. "Why don't you eat something, girl? You look like you need to be dating' Popeye with them skinny legs and big feet."

Lynette would then get wind of what he had said and she would promptly curse him out and a battle would ensue. "Nigga, I told you not to be talking to my child like that. There is nothing wrong with her hair. It's thick, coarse, and beautiful, and I'm not going to have you make her feel bad about it. You need to tell that baby mama of yours to do something with that stringy-haired child of yours and leave my baby alone. Just because she's got wavy hair don't mean she cute!" Jerome would retaliate and the argument wouldn't end, usually, until Andrew would yell at them both to shut up all the noise.

Ayanna seemed to be the only one who had excitement in her life and was very happy (which Jerome despised). She had found more than just her father and brother. She had gained a whole new family. Two weeks after their meeting, Eddie and Ayanna went to see Cedric, who was two years older than his sister. Lynette had to drop Ayanna off because Eddie hadn't been allowed on Andrew's property ever since he found out how his daughter had been treated during her pregnancy.

"Nigga, if I ever see you again, I swear I'll shoot you so short you'll be walking on your elbows," had been his exact words.

Lynette hadn't been pleased with the outcome of Ayanna's and Eddie's meeting, but she patiently listened and gritted her teeth as Ayanna went on and on daily about her paternal family. Ayanna had instantly fallen in love with her brother

Cedric. She talked non-stop about how he was teaching her how to play the piano and how he had shown her off to his friends in the neighborhood. Her adolescent chest puffed up when she told Lynette that Cedric had told his friends that they would have to deal with him if they ever messed with his little sister. Sheila had even taken Ayanna with her and Cedric to church. Though Lynette admitted to herself only that she admired Sheila for it, she didn't trust her still.

Ayanna had also met her grandmother Rose and her aunts Diane and Evelyn, Uncle Anthony and a host of cousins. She could hardly contain her excitement when she told her mother how she and her cousins Mia, Anita, and Kaley played dress-up and pretended they were the Pointer Sisters, singing "Yes We Can Can" over their grandmother's house. Ayanna had many wonderful stories, so much that Lynette couldn't help but feel a twinge of jealousy. Ayanna hadn't mentioned her father and Lynette never asked. She didn't want them to meet in the first place. There would be peace between her and Eddie as long as Ayanna was happy.

It was getting close to Ayanna's twelfth birthday. She had been asking for a boom-box and the Janet Jackson "Control" cassette tape as well as the group Cameo for some time. Lynette decided to take a trip over to Eddie's and have him give her the money for them. "Hell, he claims the he wants to make it up to Ayanna." Lynette grumbled to herself on the drive over. "Let him buy her birthday gifts."

She finally arrived at his house but no one was there. As she was walking back to her car, someone called out to her.

"Excuse me, pretty lady?"

Lynette turned to where the voice was coming from. There was an old man with a gray tint to his skin as if he hadn't taken a sip of water a day in his life. He was standing by the building next to Eddie's. He gave Lynette a toothless smile. "Don't mean to bother you. My name's Ben. You're looking for Eddie though, ain't you?"

"Yes sir." Lynette replied, trying to be respectful of her elders no matter how dirty they were.

"I saw him leaving 'bout an hour ago in his uniform. He's on his way to work, I'm guessing."

Lynette nodded. "Thank you. I'm going to go find him now."

She was almost to the car when he called out to her again. "I saw you a couple times dropping off your lil' girl. You got a pretty lil' girl, ya know." The old man chuckled and spit on the ground.

Lynette spun around. She didn't want any man looking at her daughter; especially this dirty old man standing not ten feet away from her. She quickly shortened the distance between them. "I'm going to tell you this one time so you'd better take heed. Don't you ever look at my daughter again and don't let me find out you were anywhere near her. You'll be missing a lot more than teeth." She stared into his shocked eyes for one final moment before she turned around, stomped to her car, and sped away in search of Eddie, she now had plenty to say to him.

Lynette was furious as she drove through the gates of the Waste Water Treatment Plant. Eddie had worked there before Lynette met him. She had visited him on occasion when they were dating, so she knew where to find him. Having found Eddie in such a condition, she doubted if he had moved up the ladder at work. When she had found her way to the purifying area, she discovered that she had been correct.

There he was, sitting in a chair in the corner with his long legs stretched out in front of him; same legs as her daughter. Arms were folded across his chest while his head drooped to the side. He was fast asleep.

"Look at this Nigga." Lynette thought. "What did I ever see in him?" She walked over and hit him on the leg. "Eddie!"

Eddie jumped up so quickly, he knocked over the chair that he was sitting in. It took him a moment to focus on Lynette. "Damn, Lynette! What are you doing here?"

Lynette put both hands on her hips. "I came here to discuss something with you about your daughter. Why else would I be here?"

Eddie ran his hand over his head and sighed. "Damn, woman. Why you always got to be so mean? What's going on with Ayanna that's so important that you had to come up to my job?"

"First of all, I'm only mean when I'm around you because I can't stand you for obvious reasons, which I won't bother to get into with you. Second, I went by your place before I came here. I knew you were here because of your neighbor who saw you leaving in your uniform." Lynette said with attitude. "Speaking of which…I don't want that bastard near my daughter or even looking in her direction, and I've already let him know."

"Lynette, what are you….?"

"He made a comment about Ayanna." Lynette interrupted. "Saying how pretty she is. I don't play when it comes to my baby. I know how men think and I will hold you responsible if some shit goes down."

"This woman has lost her mind." Eddie thought.

"Lynette, you are talking crazy. I wouldn't let nobody hurt Ayanna. If they tried, they'd be a dead dog."

The statement did little to calm Lynette down but it made her give Eddie the benefit of the doubt. "As long as we have an understanding. I don't like the way that man sounds and looks"

Eddie walked over to check the water levels. "So, is that all you wanted to talk to me about? I can handle that."

"No." Lynette picked up the fallen chair and sat down. "That's not all."

"Well, what's going on?"

"Ayanna's birthday is coming up in November, which I'm sure you didn't remember, seeing as you've never bothered to come around. She's been wanting a boom-box and some new tapes for a while but I just haven't been able to get anything extra. I came to see what kind of money you're working with. I've been doing it all of these years, so now it's your turn."

"I knew it was coming sooner or later." Eddie thought. "Uh...yeah....yeah." Eddie stuttered. "How much you think you need?"

Lynette shrugged. "I don't know, Eddie. Give me a hundred dollars. That should do it." She waited for his reaction to her dollar amount.

Eddie quickly turned his head away from Lynette. "Alright. I don't have it with me. Why don't you go ahead and get her presents and I'll give it back to you."

Lynette saw right through him. "Nigga, there's no need to stall. You either got it or you don't."

Eddie quickly got defensive. "I just don't have it on me, woman. Just come by my place on Friday evening. I'll have the money then." He was ready for Lynette to go so he could go back to taking his nap. Between her and Sheila, they were driving Eddie crazy. Both women were making demands on him daily concerning his children. So much pressure that he was ready to get a vasectomy to prevent any future mishaps.

"Okay, Eddie. I'm going to give you the benefit of the doubt. I'll be over at your place at six o'clock on Friday." She started to leave but suddenly remembered her encounter with the old man. "Don't forget about what I said earlier about your neighbor. I don't trust him and I don't want him anywhere near my daughter. He'd better keep on walking if he sees her. If you can't handle that, then you don't need to have her over."

Eddie watched her as she walked out of the room. "Damn. What have I gotten myself into?" He said to no one in particular and eased himself back down on the chair to continue his nap.

*****

"Lil' gal!" Andrew yelled from the back porch. "I said, lil' gal, where you at?" He pressed on.

Lynette heard her father yelling from her room. She put down her favorite book and went outside to where Andrew was standing on the porch looking annoyed.

"I said lil' gal! Where is she?" Andrew demanded.

"She's with her father's people, daddy."

Andrew's eyes narrowed. "What father? What people? All she got is us."

"That's why I didn't tell you sooner, daddy. Eddie and Ayanna met a couple months ago. I drop her off sometimes and she's met some of her other people." Lynette said in a huff. She didn't understand why she had to explain herself.

"Months? I should have been heard about this." Andrew

pondered the new information for a moment. Finally, he simply stated, "Well, at least he knows not to come around here. He'd have a buckshot in his ass if he did."

"I know, daddy. I let her go over there because it makes her happy. I don't like it, though. I was hoping she'd be tired of his sorry ass by now." She smacked her lips. "Do you know I went over there last week to get some money for Ayanna's birthday present? But he was only able to give me twenty dollars. He gave me some sorry excuse about his money being tight this week. I wanted to slap the hell out of him again. What is twenty dollars going to do?"

Andrew just shook his head. "In my day (Lynette rolled her eyes) men didn't just abandon their children. We did right by them. If you didn't, then you'd best believe you'd get a good talking to by your friends and family. You get no respect like that, see?" Andrew started walking to his tool shed with Lynette following him.

"Well, daddy, men aren't what they used to be"

"It's the way they are raised, now. Mamas don't be disciplining them right and they go out in the world and act a fool. And you women ain't no better." Andrew cut his eyes at his daughter.

"What do you mean? What are we doing wrong?"

"You women don't know how to pick good men these days. You go for the money and them fancy cars, and these niggas ain't worth two cents. I knew when I met that young fella, he wasn't no damn good. Hell, a blind man could see that two states away. But for some strange reason, you couldn't."

Lynette looked down at her feet. She felt like she had just got her hand caught in the cookie jar. "He was just something to do daddy." No sooner had the words escaped her lips, Lynette regretted them.

"Something to do!" Andrew threw up his hands. "Something to do!" He repeated. "Something got done alright. You're raisin lil' gal on your own and now you mad at the child's daddy when you need to be mad at yourself too for getting involved with that bum!"

"I know, daddy," was all Lynette could manage.

Andrew knew his daughter was under a lot of stress and he softened his tone. "Look gal, I just don't wanna see you hurt no more, that's all. It's different when a man's got daughters. I was lucky. I had your mama….." He broke off.

Lynette felt a wave of love and compassion for her father. "You're right, daddy. I've got to do better. I'm going to hit some stores and see where I can get my child this boom-box without it breaking me."

"Here." Andrew reached into his back pocket and retrieved his wallet.

"Oh no. You don't need to give me anything." Lynette quickly spoke up. But, she couldn't help but get angry at the fact that Ayanna's own father wouldn't reach into his back pocket as quickly.

"Gal, this is my money so don't tell me what the hell I don't need to do with it. Don't get sassy. Now take this money." Andrew demanded as he handed Lynette a crisp fifty-dollar bill. "Get my grandbaby that boom thing."

"Thank you, daddy. Boom-box." Lynette said as she kissed him on the cheek. "I love you."

"Humph." Was Andrew's reply as she bounced away but not before she saw the hint of a smile.

Sixth Chapter

"Eddie, I want to go over to Aunt Diane's house." Ayanna was tired of being cooped up in her father's place. She never liked being in this tiny house with dishes in the sink that were never washed, and dirty magazines peeking from underneath the pillows on the sofa. Ayanna was always getting on Eddie about cleaning up because her mother kept their home spotless, even with her uncle tracking dirt through it on purpose. Eddie would just glance around for a moment and then say he would get to it later. She got up from the kitchen table and stood next to Eddie who was on the sofa watching television.

He looked over at Ayanna. "You don't want to stay here and hang out with your old man? I got some cards in the room. I can teach you some Spades."

Ayanna didn't want to hurt his feelings but she wasn't about to stay where she was either. "Me and Anita were supposed to hang out. Plus, I wanted to go to church with them tomorrow."

Eddie looked at Ayanna a moment before turning back to the television. "How you gonna make plans with them when you're supposed to be hanging out with me? Your old man." He paused for a minute and then threw up his hands in frustration. "Never mind. Alright. When you trying to go over there?"

"Can we go now?" Ayanna asked a little too eagerly for Eddie's taste. She quickly added, "That way, me and Anita can hang outside while it's still light. Aunt Diane don't like us out when it's dark."

"Nothing's out there after dark for you two anyway." Eddie didn't want to take Ayanna over to his sister's house so soon. He had hoped to be able to spend some more time with her. He had been unable to really reach her since they met and he was beginning to lose hope. He had even cut back on his heroine intake so he could be himself with Ayanna and have some fun. Unfortunately, she only wanted to spend time with her brother and cousins.

"Get your coat, Ayanna. We can go now if you want to. Your aunt knows you're coming?" Eddie asked knowing the answer already.

Ayanna was already putting on her coat. "Yes, she knows." She answered.

"Damn, can she move any faster?" Eddie thought, watching Ayanna gather her bags at the speed of light. "Hell, I need a fix anyway. A nigga need a little pep in his step." He got up and turned off the television before grabbing his own coat.

"You can stay over there until church is out. I know everybody's going to be over your grandma's house so I'll pick you up from over there." He grabbed her suitcase. "You cool with that?"

"Yeah, that's cool, Eddie." Ayanna answered as he opened the door.

Eddie flinched. He wished she could feel comfortable

enough to call her dad. "What? I can't get a Pop or Old Man?" He asked.

Ayanna looked back at him like he was crazy. "I'm not ready for that yet." She stated in a matter-of-fact manner.

"Damn, she's just like her mama." Eddie thought. "I'll just have to try a little harder."

They headed towards Eddie's father, George's, house where Diane was living. Their father had died two years earlier. Right after the funeral, Diane hosted the dinner for the family at his house and to no one's surprise, she simply never left. Ayanna loved going there. It was a tri-level house with a huge front and back yard. It used to have the prettiest lawn in the neighborhood with rose bushes surrounding the house, which George meticulously took care of when he was alive. Now, the rose bushes were dead and the grass would only be cut when the neighbors shouted at Diane to do something about it. She would tell them to go to hell and stomp away, but the next day the grass would always be cut.

Ayanna and her cousin, Anita, would skate around in the basement or play dress-up in the attic with their grandmother's ancient clothes. Those were the times she cherished most. Her aunt was always acting silly and Ayanna loved how spunky she was. Her mom was always working, so she didn't get to spend a lot of time with Ayanna. Plus, with a grandfather who drank too much and an uncle who despised her at home, there wasn't much room for being silly.

Eddie glanced over at Ayanna who seemed to be deep in thought. "Care to share what's on your mind?"

Ayanna snapped out of her trance. "Huh? Oh nothing."

Eddie tried a different approach. "Hey, I know how much

you like seafood. How about we go to Captain George's and then catch a movie for your birthday."

Ayanna loved Captain George's. Her mother would take her there from time to time as a special treat for both of them. She had never gone with anyone else but she figured she would try with Eddie. It might be fun. "Okay, we can do that." Was her simple reply.

Eddie inwardly breathed a sigh of relief. "Good, I'll let your mama know and we can work out the time and all that."

They rode in silence for a while until they reached Diane's. Eddie put the car in the park situated in front of the house while leaving the motor running. He gently placed his hands-on top of Ayanna's. "Remember Ayanna that if you need me you can just call. You got the number. If not, I'll just pick you up at your grandma's house after church. She throws down every Sunday so I'm gonna come on an empty stomach."

Ayanna did not like the feeling of her father touching her. She slowly slid her hand from underneath Eddie's. Discomfort was written all over her face which did not go unnoticed.

"I'm sorry, baby girl. I didn't mean to make you uncomfortable." Eddie didn't know how he should take her reaction. "Does she really think that I would do anything to hurt her?"

"It's okay." Ayanna replied as he unlocked her door. "I'll just see you tomorrow at Grandma Rose's house." She got out and waved goodbye before running up to the front door.

"Hey!" Eddie yelled. "Tell your aunt and cousin I said hey and I'll see them tomorrow."

Ayanna nodded her head and knocked on the door. When it opened, Eddie drove off. The last thing he saw in his rearview mirror was Ayanna still standing in the same spot staring in his direction.

Eddie headed straight for Sweetman's house in the West End. Sweetman, whose legal name was Christopher Johnson, was the go-to-man for any high-quality drug of choice. His drugs were of the greatest quality and would have any unsuspecting addict on the verge of losing their home, car, and family. But Sweetman was very discreet and only sold to his regulars through his various employees. This helped to avoid compromising his business, while ensuring imminent death for any foolish man or woman who dared to open their mouths to the wrong person. You would never guess that this 5'5", dark-skinned, extremely obese man with coke-bottle glasses and who was a full-time tax attorney, was one of the most respected drug dealers in the South East.

Eddie had been getting marijuana, coke, and occasionally heroin from him for years. He was one of Sweetman's most loyal customers; a fact that Eddie was secretly ashamed of. Sweetman would give Eddie drugs on credit from time to time, because he knew that Eddie would always come back for more or put in some work. As Eddie pulled into the new development that Sweetman lived in, he knew in his gut that he needed to turn around. But, the stress and shame of having his daughter in his life and seeing him this way kept him driving forward, literally, straight to his dealer. "What was the harm in taking off the edge a little?" He could already feel the sweet sensation of the calmness enveloping him. He would be able to face his poor excuse for a life just a little while longer.

He finally spotted the huge two-story brick house with a blue Ford Taurus in the driveway. Sweetman was never one to bring attention to himself. Eddie parked at the end of the block as required by Sweetman. Eddie then proceeded to the side entrance. He knocked once and paused. He knocked twice and paused again. And then he knocked three times. After a moment of silence, he heard the slight buzz of a camera but he couldn't see it. The door clicked open and Eddie walked in. He was standing in a hug den with a fireplace taking up half of the wall. The room was decorated with soft earth-tones and plaques of Sweetman's achievements in the legal world were hanging on one side of the wall, as well as huge bay windows on the other. Sweetman was sitting behind his cherry wood desk with Big Mike, his right-hand man, standing beside him with his hands folded in front of him.

"Eddie, my man." Sweetman stood up to greet Eddie. "How have you been? I don't see you as much these days. Are you going clean on me?" He looked over at Big Mike and winked.

Eddie chuckled nervously. "I'm doing my best, man. I've been trying to stay straight for my daughter."

Sweetman raised his eyebrows. "Daughter? I didn't know you had a daughter. I just thought you had little junior." He said, puzzled.

"Yeah, well, me and her mama… don't… I mean… didn't really get along. She only brought my daughter to see me a few months ago." His tone then changed to almost pleading. "I've been doing good man but I need a little help right now. She doesn't even look at me like I'm a man and I'm her father." Eddie looked away and shoved his hands deep into his pockets.

Sweetman gestured for Big Mike to bring him his Cuban cigars and matches. He never used a lighter because he said it took away from the rich taste of the cigar. There was silence in the room except for the strike of the match and the slow burning leaves as Sweetman inhaled. "Come and have a seat." Sweetman said, gesturing to Eddie to join him on the plush cream-colored sectional. It was rare for him to allow anyone to come to his house to make a transaction. This was limited only to a few who had been loyal to him for years. He would view everything from his private office thanks to the many hidden cameras spread throughout his house. It was always the first business he tended to whenever he purchased new homes. Security could never be too tight for Sweetman. But he somewhat liked Eddie; and even had something special in store for him. Sweetman had known Eddie when he was just a young thug on the streets. Eddie had been excellent with numbers and could out-hustle the best. Sweetman had already offered to bring him to his team if he agreed to clean himself up. Eddie was now overdue with his answer.

"Have you thought about my proposition?" Sweetman asked as he took a puff of his cigar.

Eddie's eyes darted from Sweetman to Big Mike and back again. "I've thought about it."

Sweetman smiled coyly. "Well, what's your answer, my man? I don't like to keep my money waiting. I've got soldiers in Fairfield and Mosby Court. Also, I've got a few in Wickham. I want you to make sure the money always adds up and the supply always meets the demand. My blocks should never be dry. Can you handle that or are you afraid of being caught up?"

Eddie was silent for a moment. This was the hustle that he had been referring to when Lynette first showed up on his doorstep. He leaned forward. "So I wouldn't have to really handle the product?" He was never one to get his hands dirty.

"No." Sweetman answered. "I've got a series of runners that rotate. You report what product and how much is needed on the blocks to my people and they handle it from there. If the money my soldiers made doesn't add up with the amount of product given to them, my people need to know that too. So what do you say? It's my final offer." Sweetman continued to puff on his cigar as he waited for an answer. Meanwhile, Big Mike was glaring at Eddie with a smirk on his face.

Eddie didn't appreciate how Big Mike was looking at him but he kept this thought to himself. "I have thought about it." Eddie sat up straighter. "I'm going to have to take you up on your offer. I need the money and niggas know me from back in the day."

Sweetman crossed his legs and pointed the burning cigar at Eddie. "I don't want nonsense. I run my business how I run my business and I won't have my rules broken."

"Rules?" Eddie asked.

"I don't employ junkies." Sweetman answered in a serious tone; cutting right to the chase. "Bad for business in my line of work, you see."

Eddie looked over at Big Mike who was still glaring at him with his arms folded. "Why is this beefed up bastard eye-balling me?" Eddie was sick of Sweetman's side-kick trying to intimidate him. "Sweetman, I know what you're saying." Eddie said as he focused back on business. "I need this so I can provide for my little man and my daughter. I can quit, easily."

"Good. Good. That's what I want to hear." Sweetman smiled and tapped Big Mike on the arm who promptly left the room. "I'm going to have my men send instructions to your house."

"You know where I stay?" Eddie asked only a little surprised. He did not know Sweetman made it his business to know everything about the people he dealt with.

Sweetman chuckled. "Man, of course I do. I'm always kept well informed."

Big Mike walked back in the room with a small wooden box and set it on the glass table in front of Eddie. Sweetman slapped him on the back. "Of course, I don't see why you can't indulge one last time." He said, lifting the lid and revealing the white powder. "I see you're going through some things so go ahead and help yourself to a few lines. I'm not sending you home with any, though."

Eddie couldn't have been happier. "Thanks man. I really appreciate it. I really do."

Sweetman became silent and leaned back on the couch. Through the haze of cigar smoke, Sweetman watched as Eddie prepared to fly.

Seventh Chapter

Lynette couldn't believe how handsome he was. Why did she have to be in this raggedy Safeway uniform with her hair pulled back in a pony-tail and no makeup on? On today of all times? Paula, her coworker, had called in sick and Lynette had been asked to come in on her night off to fill in for a few hours. She hadn't had time to spruce herself up. She was working the cash register and had seen this tall stocky man picking out some canned goods. She loved the way his jeans hugged him just right, and she could see that his arms were well-toned underneath his baby blue cardigan sweater.

"Excuse me, miss? Are you open?" Asked an elderly woman with a cart full of groceries.

Lynette hadn't been paying attention to the waiting woman. "Oh, yes mam. I'm so sorry. I can ring you up." Lynette started ringing up the items at lightning speed. She didn't want the handsome man to go to another line that was shorter.

"My goodness, you're fast." The old woman said in awe. She then caught sight of Lynette's distraction and the reason for her speedy work. "My. My. I can see why you're trying to get rid of me." She said with a twinkle in her eye.

Lynette just blushed. "Oh no mam. I'm not rushing you." She said, embarrassed that she was so obvious.

The woman laughed. "Honey, I'm only messing with you."

Lynette thanked her and finished ringing up her groceries. After the woman had paid for her groceries at the pace of a turtle, Lynette looked up and saw the mysterious man searching lines.

"I can take you over here sir." Lynette eagerly called out. "Hell, I'll take you anywhere." she thought mischievously.

He flashed her a smile with a set of perfect white teeth. Lynette loved a man with pretty teeth.

"So how are you doing today?" He asked in a sexy baritone voice as he walked up to her register.

Lynette self-consciously smoothed back her hair and smiled back shyly at him. "I'm fine and you?"

"Well…." He paused and looked around. "I'm much better now, thank you, since I'm in the presence of such a beautiful lady."

Lynette wasn't expecting that statement at all. Was he flirting with her? It had been so long, she didn't think she could recognize it if it was happening. He couldn't be. Not today, with the way she looked. "Well, thank you, but you must have cataracts or something because I look a mess today."

He laughed at her statement. To Lynette, it was like music. "Damn, even his laugh is sexy." She thought.

"I can tell that you're something else." He stated when he stopped laughing. "My name is Marcus."

"Nice to meet you, Marcus. I'm Lynette."

"Well, Lynette. I've been here a few times before in the last few months and I've seen you here working. You're always so busy so I've never really had a chance to talk to you." He leaned a little closer and Lynette had to catch her breath. "I think that you're prettier without makeup. But that's just my opinion."

Lynette swore to never wear makeup again if it meant getting to know Marcus better. She blushed. "Marcus, are you flirting with me?"

He flashed her another brilliant smile. "It depends on if it's helping me to get you to go out with me for dinner. What do you say?"

Lynette pretended like she was thinking about it, but the truth was that she was already picking out her outfit in her head. "Well, why not? It might be fun. Here, I'll give you my number and you give me a call." Lynette said as she scribbled her number on a paper bag.

Marcus put the number in his wallet. "I always guarantee a good time. Don't worry."

"Good. But I hope you don't plan on cooking for me at home with all these canned goods you've got here." Lynette chuckled as she rang up his items.

"Oh no. I will make sure I take you somewhere worthier."

Lynette handed him his paper bags. "Well, I guess I'll be talking to you soon, I hope."

Marcus looked at her for a moment. "You can count on it."

Lynette watched him walking out of the store. "Thank you, God, for creatures like that. Your works are wonderful indeed." She was so lost in her thoughts that she barely heard the clearing of several throats of customers in her line waiting to be rang up. With a sheepish smile and an apology, Lynette got back to work.

*****

True to his word, Marcus called three days later. They had talked for two hours and would have talked much longer if Andrew hadn't started to complain about Lynette laughing loudly on the phone.

"Gal, cut out all that damn racket! I'm tryin' to get me some rest!" He yelled.

Lynette sighed. Why couldn't she ever get some peace? "Marcus, I'm about to get off this phone but I've really enjoyed our conversation.

"So have I, Lynette." Michael said with disappointment at her cutting their conversation short. "I could listen to your voice all night."

Lynette closed her eyes. "This man is going to make me tear his sexy ass up when I see him." She thought. "I appreciate that, Marcus but, we've got to save something to talk about when we go out Friday night. Food can only occupy us for a little while, you know."

"Alright, Lynette, don't forget to meet me at Red Lobster on West Broad Street at eight o'clock. I don't know why you won't just let me pick you up? Don't let me find out that I'm going to have to fight for your love because you've got somebody at home." Marcus said playfully.

Lynette laughed. "Please. I definitely don't have any prospects here. Besides, you could be a serial killer. A girl's got to be cautious and my mama didn't raise no fool."

"Well, we'll soon change that attitude. Just don't stand me up. I'll see you soon and sleep well, Lynette."

"In your own words Marcus...you can count on it."

Lynette had wonderful thoughts of Marcus and their conversation earlier. It had been a long time since she met someone whose mind was just as appealing as his body. She could hardly wait for her date just three days away. She would ask her sister, Catheryn, to watch Ayanna. Ayanna was her favorite of all the nieces and nephews and Catheryn didn't mind sharing that fact. She had been told numerous times that she shouldn't play favorites but, Catheryn didn't care. Yani was her baby, she would always say. So, Lynette knew she would not have trouble finding a babysitter. She and Marcus had talked about almost everything. She had been pleased when she found out he owned his own private rig, which he contracted for big companies like Nabisco and Phillip Morris. He was a savvy business man but, unfortunately, resided in Charlotte North Carolina. He was divorced at thirty with two small girls, ages eight and ten that he actually had full custody of. Lynette had listened in amazement as Marcus had recounted how he and the girls' mother, Shannon, had met in the ninth grade. Marcus played football and Shannon had been a cheerleader. They soon became a handsome couple. It was classic jock and popular girl love. Shannon had a deep chocolate complexion, almond eyes, and wavy jet-black hair that hung past her shoulders (compliments of West Indian maternal grandparents). Marcus was already six feet tall with curly hair and skin the color of cinnamon. He was the star running-back for the school's undefeated football team. They had courted all through high school and both went on to attend University of North Caroline in Charlotte.

Things went well their freshman year but by the beginning of their sophomore year, the couple became careless and Shannon became pregnant. Marcus was going to school on a full academic scholarship. His grandmother had always said that if your body gave out, you would have to have your mind to fall back on. He had studied and worked hard and was on his way to becoming very successful. But, Marcus had to do the right thing. He and Shannon were married in her fourth month of pregnancy at the Justice of the Peace. Shannon became Mrs. Shannon Martel-Scott and continued school until her eighth month and Marcus dropped out of school to work full time for a prominent trucking company as a driver, making a low five-figure salary. To say that both of their families were disappointed was an understatement. But, Marcus being one of the best drivers, even amongst the veterans, and smart with money (thanks once again to the teachings of his grandmother); soon provided the home and lifestyle a young married couple could be proud of.

When their daughter, Sinai, was a year and a half, Shannon became pregnant again. Up until this time, she had been a stay-at-home mother. She had planned on seeking a job as a paralegal when Sinai was two and would be comfortable in a daycare. Marcus took more out-of-state jobs, which would almost double his regular salary, to prepare for the new arrival. By the time the couple's second daughter, Ciara, was born, Marcus's time at home was practically non-existent. Shannon became lonelier and more resentful as the years passed by with no one but the girls to keep her company. Pleas to Marcus resulted in him working less for a month or two before he would go right back to being a workaholic.

One night, Marcus returned home from a two-week assignment and found bags and suitcases by the front door. An argument ensued between Marcus and Shannon when she informed him that she was leaving to pursue her career, and she had no room for him or the girls in her life at the moment. She left and never looked back.

As Lynette reflected on the intimate details that Marcus has shared with her, she couldn't help but admire and respect him for taking such good care of his girls. She could hear the pride and love in his voice when he talked about them. This just made him all the more appealing to Lynette.

"Why am I so smitten with this man that I just met?" Lynette asked herself.

Maybe it was the fact that, since Eddie, Lynette had never really trusted another man with her feelings. She had also wanted to spend as much time as she could with Ayanna and thus didn't have the energy for men and their games. But Ayanna was getting older and was venturing out more and more on her own. Lynette was ready to get her feet wet again (and possibly some other body parts) and have some fun in her life.

"Yes," Lynette thought aloud as she inspected the outfits she had lain on her bed. "I'm going to start having a good time and Marcus is just the person to do it with."

"Mama, I like the red one better." Ayanna was lying across her mother's bed watching her try on different outfits. It was finally Friday.

Lynette sighed as she looked in the mirror for what seemed like the hundredth time. "No baby, it makes me look like a hooker. "Lynette answered absentmindedly.

"A hooker?"

Lynette realized what she said. "I'm sorry, baby. What I mean is that I want to look like a classy lady and this red just won't do it. You'll understand when you get older."

"Everybody always says that. I can't wait to get older." Ayanna pouted.

Lynette looked at her daughter through the mirror. "Don't wish yourself older, Yani. Once you get there, you're going to wish you were young again."

"I don't see why, mama. Grownups get to do all the fun stuff like go out to parties and fancy dinners when they want to. Kids don't have any rights."

Lynette burst out laughing and turned to Ayanna. "Rights? Girl, I'll tell you what rights you have. You have the right to eat and sleep with a roof over your head for free until you're eighteen. You have the right to clothes on your back which I could easily give some other child who appreciates them. You have the right to a free education. Do you want me to go on child about your lack of rights?"

Ayanna didn't respond.

"Ummmhmmm." Lynette said as she turned back to the mirror. "Your aunt Catheryn will be here soon. Do you have your bags packed? And you know you need to pack at least two pairs of extra clothing or she'll declare to the family that I'm an unfit mother."

Ayanna giggled.

"It's not funny, Ayanna." Lynette said as she giggled despite herself at the way her sister always blew things out of proportion.

"Aunt Catheryn always says you have to be prepared because anything could come up." Ayanna said with the hint of a smile on her lips.

Lynette rolled her eyes. "Humph. The only place you all ever go is to the grocery store and next door to nosey old Ms. Betsy's house. She'll be here in a minute, anyway, so let me hurry up before I hear her mouth."

Lynette quickly put on a baby-blue dress with spaghetti straps, a fitted waist, and it flared out at the bottom which ended right above the knee. She finished it off with the baby-blue sling-back pumps with beige heels and matching purse.

She wore a simple pearl necklace and dainty pearl earrings. She stepped back and admired herself in the mirror and smiled.

"Mama, you look gorgeous!" Ayanna stared at her mother in awe.

Lynette couldn't help but grin from ear to ear. "Thank you, baby. I hope you're not the only one who thinks so." She turned back to her reflection. "Damn, I do look good." She thought.

She looked at the clock on her nightstand. It was six-thirty. Catheryn was supposed to be there to pick Ayanna up by seven. That way Lynette could be on the road by seven-fifteen and have enough time to not have to rush. "Alright, chop chop." Lynette said as she snapped her fingers. "You gather your stuff, young lady, and bring it in the den. I'm going to make you a chicken salad sandwich to take with you. You know your aunt can't cook."

Ayanna's face lit up. She loved her mother's homemade chicken salad. "Thanks mama. I won't take too long."

Lynette smiled and looked at her daughter one last time before leaving the room. God only knew how much she loved her little girl. She would do anything to ensure her happiness. She went down to the kitchen and found her father sitting at the table sharpening his knife.

"Hi daddy." Whatcha been up to all day?"

Andrew, who was concentrating on the blade, didn't look up. "I been out with Cleavie hunting deer. I'm about to go and get me this nice big one from out the cooler that I just shot. You want to come, gal?"

"Daddy, how am I supposed to help get a deer in this dress?"

Andrew looked up at Lynette for the first time since she had entered the kitchen.

"Gal is you goin out prosecutin? He yelled as he slammed down his knife.

Lynette was confused. "Prosecutin?"

"Yes!" Andrew yelled. "You look like a prosecutor! You don't need to be going nowhere dressed like that. Plus you got a child gal. She don't need to see her mother dressed that way and I mean it."

"Prosecutor. Prosecutor." Lynette mumbled to herself until it dawned on her what her meant and what he was trying to say. "Daddy do you mean prostitute?"

Andrew was now beet red. "Gal don't get sassy with me. I'm going to tell you one last time that a woman with a child shouldn't be walking around like that. No telling what men are thinking." Andrew fumed.

"Daddy I am grown! There is nothing wrong with what I have on. I'm going out and have me a good time." Lynette was tired of her father being judgmental.

"And who's going to take care of Yani while you off running in the damn streets?"

Lynette glanced out of the window. "For your information, Catheryn is keeping Ayanna tonight and I am not running the streets. I work hard and I deserve to have fun just as much as the next person. Now leave me alone daddy. I'm trying to finish up her so I can get to where I need to be on time." Lynette set about preparing Ayanna's sandwich.

Andrew continued to ramble on about "a woman's place" until Jerome stormed into the kitchen demanding to know what the noise was.

"What's going on here? I'm trying to get some damn rest

before my night shift!" Jerome shouted with red unfocused eyes fixed on Lynette.

"Don't look at me. "Lynette threw up her hands. "Talk to daddy. I just came in here to make Ayanna a sandwich and he started with me about my dress." Lynette replied before putting her hands on her hips for emphasis.

Jerome looked at his sister from head to toe. "Well you do look like a whore." He simply stated with no expression at all.

Lynette was shocked. "Fuck you Jerome!" She screamed. "You just mad because you with that wilder beast. I'd be mad too if I had to kiss that."

Jerome turned a bright shade of purple and got in his sister's face. "Who the fuck do you think you talking to. There's nothing wrong with Liza. At least she's not out whorin' in the street and leaving her child with different people all the time."

Lynette was on fire now. "You don't know what the hell you're talking about. I work two damn jobs while school is in session and I take damn good care of my daughter and this house. If I want to leave Ayanna with her family then I will. I deserve to go out as much as you do. I don't see you with your daughter very often. What about that? Take your high and mighty ass out my face Jerome and leave me alone."

Lynette started to turn back to the sandwich when her brother's hands were suddenly around her throat. She screamed as she reached up to try to release his strong grip.

Andrew jumped up from his chair. "Now son...."

"Stay out of this old man!" Jerome snapped.

Ayanna had heard the commotion and had come running into the kitchen. "Uncle Jerome get your hands off my mama!" She screamed.

Hands still around Lynette's throat, Jerome cast a steely glance at Ayanna. "Stay out of this Boney before I backhand you."

"Ayanna," Lynette gasped. "Get out of here." She was still struggling to get out of her brother's grasp.

"What do I do? What do I do?" Ayanna thought as she looked around for anything she could find to get her uncle off her mom. She spotted the knife on the kitchen table and grabbed it. Her hands were shaking uncontrollably.

"Get off my mama before I cut you!" Ayanna raised the knife in the air and gripped it tighter. She was tired of her uncle's evil ways and she was determined to make him bleed if she could.

Jerome looked at Ayanna a moment before letting his sister go. He sneered at Ayanna and got closer to her. "What do you think you're going to do huh? You're gonna cut me? Let me see what you've got tough girl." He taunted.

Lynette had finally been able to catch her breath. "Leave her alone you son of a bitch." Then she addressed Ayanna. "Ayanna, I told you to get out of here."

Andrew had been frozen in shock. He finally regained his voice. "Come on lil' gal. You don't need to be around this."

"Yes, I do granddaddy!" Ayanna was near hysteria. She lunged towards her uncle as he attempted to take away the knife. He accidentally grabbed the blade and blood quickly started pouring from his hand.

"Oh shit!" Jerome moaned as he sat down and Lynette grabbed a cloth, more out of concern for her clean tiled floor than her brother's well-being, and wrapped it around his hand.

"Put some pressure on it!" Lynette commanded. She looked at Ayanna who was standing in the same place and her eyes were fixed on her uncle with the knife still in her hand.

"Give me the knife baby. It's okay." Lynette spoke softly to her trying to coax the knife from her hands. She didn't want to set her off in any way.

"Knock knock. Coming in!" Catheryn was coming up the back porch. She opened the screen door and came in not knowing what lay just inside. "Hey everybody. Ayanna, baby, you ready to...?" She trailed off when she spotted the knife in Ayanna's hand and took a really good look at the scene that had just unfolded. Jerome had a blood-soaked cloth wrapped around his hand and Lynette was rubbing her neck. Andrew was sitting in a chair looking weary and much older than his normal age.

"What the hell is going on here?" Catheryn still had one hand gripping the doorknob. She thought that, surely, her eyes were deceiving her.

"Hell, if you got eyes, you can see what's going on woman. Don't you see that child with a knife in her hand and me over here bleeding? Jerome was beginning to look weak.

Catheryn turned to Ayanna. "Ayanna what in the world were you thinking? Why would you cut your uncle? That's your flesh and blood." Catheryn stretched out her hand. "Give me the knife." When she saw how Ayanna tightened her grip on the knife without saying a word, Catheryn decided to use a different approach. She lowered her voice and spoke lovingly. "Yani? It's okay. Give me the knife baby." She stretched out her hand again and softly repeated that everything would be okay over and over again, hoping to get through to her niece. Ayanna finally slowly turned and handed the knife to her aunt and started crying.

Lynette started towards her daughter but Catheryn held

up her hand. "I've got this Netty. I'm going to take her out of this mess." Ayanna was clinging to her.

"I didn't do anything Catheryn. You don't even know what happened." Lynette pleaded. She just wanted her family to listen to her for change. "Jerome started talking mess about what I have on because of what he heard daddy saying, of course. Then he called me a whore and started choking me sis. I swear. Then Ayanna grabbed the knife so he would let me go and when he tried to grab it he got cut."

"I don't have time for this shit." Jerome stood up slowly, obviously annoyed and in pain. "Everybody must have forgotten that I'm up in here bleeding to death. I'm gone. I need to get this stitched up."

"Jerome, you know you are too weak to be driving yourself to the hospital. I can take you there." Catheryn was trying her best to pull herself together,

"I don't need you doing nothing for me." He looked down at Ayanna who looked him square in the eyes. Jerome inwardly shivered. "And I know you don't think I'm going to ride with her after what she just did to me? I'll find somebody to drive me."

As he was leaving the kitchen, Jerome stopped and turned back around. "And somebody owe me a night's pay. Since I can't go to work tonight. You can believe that shit." He stomped away; his heavy footsteps reverberating throughout the house.

Catheryn shook her head and looked down at Ayanna who was still glassy-eyed. "Come on Ayanna, get your bags so we can go." When Ayanna was out of earshot, Catheryn spoke to Lynette in a low and deadly tone. "I'm sick of all this mess that goes on around here. Between you running the streets and this house being full of turmoil all the damn time, my baby can't get no damn peace. I suggest you start on the road to correcting this situation or I'm going to take matters into my own hands."

Lynette narrowed her eyes, her sore neck forgotten. Are you threatening to take my child away from me? I am a damn good mother for your information and frankly I'm getting sick and tired of trying to prove that to you all the damn time."

Catheryn snorted. "Yeah when you're around."

"Who's feeding you this bullshit? Jerome?" Lynette couldn't believe what she was hearing. She was just about to open her mouth to tell her sister what she thought of her last comment when she heard Ayanna coming down the hall.

"You got everything baby?" Lynette asked when Ayanna entered the room.

"Yes mama," Was the tearful reply.

Lynette embraced her in a tight hug. "Don't you worry," She whispered. "I'm going to get us out of here. Okay?" She felt Ayanna shake her head up and down. "I love you Yani."

"I love you too mama." She walked out the door behind her aunt who hadn't bothered to say goodbye. Lynette didn't want to let her daughter go but she knew that it was best. There was no way Ayanna should be here right now. Hell, she didn't feel like going out but she wasn't staying home either.

Andrew had been sitting silent the entire time. He finally spoke. "I'm sorry Netty."

Lynette looked in her father's helpless eyes and she knew that she had to get her and Ayanna as far away as possible. She didn't want to leave Andrew, but she had to think of her daughter first.

She sighed a deep sigh from the soul. "Me too daddy. Me too."

Eighth Chapter

Lynette drove to the Red Lobster in tears. She couldn't believe what had just happened. She knew her brother had a mean streak but she never imagined he would try to physically hurt her. Weren't they supposed to be family? That's what Lynette had thought, anyway. Her face looked a mess and she didn't know how she was going to explain her tardiness or the way she looked tonight.

"Shit! Shit! Shit!" Lynette screamed with new tears streaming down her face. She pulled into the Red Lobster parking lot at 8:42. She hastily checked her hair and what was left of her makeup and hurried inside. She stood at the entrance and spotted Marcus nursing a wine bottle that looked half empty at one of the back tables.

"Can I help you miss? A petite hostess approached her out of nowhere.

"Oh no thank you." Lynette pointed in Marcus's direction. "I see my party waiting for me."

Lynette took a deep breath and walked up to Marcus who had just glanced at his watch. "Marcus, I'm so sorry I'm late. I had an emergency that came up at the last minute. Please forgive me." Lynette pleaded.

Marcus motioned for her to have a seat. "I was about to

give up on you. I thought I had been stood up." He said with a slight edge to his voice.

Lynette sat down across from him. "I would never stand you up. I can't say how sorry I am enough times. This really is unusual for me." She reached for a glass of water, gulped it down and nearly choked.

"Are you alright?" Marcus asked as he jumped up to aid Lynette.

Lynette, embarrassed by the way people were looking at her, could only hold her head down and nod in affirmation as she tried to catch her breath.

Marcus sat back down and sighed. He looked at Lynette and realized that her eyes were red and puffy. "Look, we can do this another time if you'd prefer. You really don't seem like you're up to this."

"Oh no, "Lynette sputtered. "I may have had a rough time before I came but here I am. I've been looking forward to our date all week."

"Well, I was just checking." Marcus said, still eying Lynette's puffy eyes. "I wanted to make sure that you had a good time tonight."

Lynette waved him off and gave him a reassuring smile. "I'm sure I will if I'm with you, Marcus." Lynette rubbed her hands together all of a sudden. "Now where's that waitress of ours. I'm starving."

*****

"Marcus, I swear I needed a night like this. I haven't laughed this much in years."

Lynette and Marcus were on the jazz floor of Ivory's, a popular club in downtown Richmond. It was well known for its three floors of great music and food. Each floor had a different style of music. R&B and Soul on the first floor, Jazz on the second, and Reggae on the top floor. You could smell the jerk and curry-seasoned food from blocks away. At the moment, Lynette was sipping on a Long Island Iced Tea and Marcus was sipping on a Black Russian.

"Well, you looked like you needed one." Marcus said with a twinkle in his eye. He loved how beautiful she was when she smiled. He had been determined to erase any demons that had followed her on their date.

Lynette beamed at Marcus sitting across from her. "You've got that right." She took another sip and looked at the couples on the dance floor.

Marcus followed her eyes. He had been waiting for the right moment to ask her if she wanted to dance and possibly get a little closer. He had had so much fun talking to her he hadn't minded not dancing for a while. "Do you want to dance? I'm not too shabby if I do say so myself."

Lynette instantly became nervous. She hadn't danced with any man since Michael.

Marcus sensed her hesitation. "What's wrong? You scared I'm going to dance circles around you? Pleeease." He patted Lynette on the knee and gave her a puppy-dog look that almost made her melt.

Lynette looked at the dance floor packed with couples dipping and swaying to the up-tempo beat of the music. She remembered the last time that she danced. Had it really been six years? She had tried so hard and for so long to make that tragic part of her life a blur. She had stored his laughter, smell, wittiness, the sound of his voice, his handsome face, and his love all in the deepest parts of her mind and soul. But here they were resurfacing just with the mere mention of dancing. She looked into Marcus's curious eyes. What the hell? She had almost blown her chance with Marcus once tonight. She wasn't about to make that mistake a second time.

"You know what? I'm going to take you up on your challenge. Just do me a favor and don't get mad when I show you up."

Marcus bowed and then gestured towards the dance floor. "After you madam."

Needless to say, he was an amazing dancer. Lynette could barely keep up with him. They danced and laughed until the house lights came on. Afterwards, they drove to Chimaraza Park and parked where they could overlook downtown, while talking about their past and their dreams.

"My main goal, Marcus, is to make the best life that I can for my daughter. She motivates me to want to do better. I'm planning my escape as we speak."

Marcus laid his head on the back of his headrest and closed his eyes. "When you're a kid, everything seems so simple doesn't it? Every kid wants to grow up and be a doctor, lawyer, or play sports. But as we get older, circumstances change and you have to change your priorities. I commend you for not letting your family deter you from making a better life for yourself. Don't feed into their skepticism." He went on to give her words of encouragement as Lynette listened intently.

Lynette would remember years later that when Marcus had kissed her, she had felt as if the world had come to a standstill just for the two of them.

When he finally drove Lynette back to her car, the electricity between them was undeniable. Marcus promised to call her and they would make arrangements to see each other again. And, no, it didn't matter that they lived in two different states. Lynette was hopeful that she had finally found happiness or at least caught a glimpse of it. And she agreed with Marcus that somehow, they would find a way to make it work.

Ninth Chapter

"Boy, they don't make them like they used to. That's for damn sure."

Eddie was sitting in his car watching Sweetman's street workers. He narrowed his eyes as he observed one of the young boys eyeing a woman coming out of a beauty salon. He had carelessly left his drugs unattended. Any crook or crackhead could have snatched up the bag and no one would have known until it was too late. Except Eddie.

Just as he was about to get out of his car to handle the situation, another older boy ran up to the bag and yelled at the one still gawking at the woman walking up the street. "Hey fool! Whatcha think you doing? You trying to get killed? Get yo shit straight!"

The younger boy abandoned his quest for the woman and looked at the older boy and nervously laughed. "Oh shit! Good looking out man. I saw that fine thang coming out the shop and she fucked my head all up."

"Aright man. Whatever. Just watch yo shit." The older boy chastised and went back to his block to continue with his own business.

Eddie had witnessed the scene. "I'm getting too old for this shit." Eddie thought and eased back down into his seat.

The money was good. That definitely wasn't the problem. He had been able to take Ayanna to Captain George's as he promised. Seeing the flicker of joy on her face when they pulled up to the restaurant had been priceless. She had allowed herself to be comfortable with him for a short while on her birthday. He had also been able to give Lynette money every week to help out. Lynette was suspicious about how he was getting the money but she never said anything about it. "Hell, that's all she cares about any way. She doesn't give a damn about me." He could tell her that he was shooting himself out of rockets to make money and all she would say is "That's nice nigga now hand over the money." The one thing he did know was that she didn't want him getting caught in the streets, which is exactly what had happened. She didn't want him involved in anything that could endanger Ayanna. Hell, Eddie couldn't blame her but he needed to make a better life for himself and his kids, and his daytime job wasn't cutting it. Besides, it was just temporary and he had to stay alert so he wasn't using anymore. The most he did was smoke a joint every now and then to keep his nerves together.

Sweetman had been pleased with his work so far. Eddie always kept the corners supplied and the monies were always counted correctly. He was a natural and he knew it. But Eddie didn't want it anymore. He had envisioned himself to be more at thirty-five. His sister Evelyn was an administrative assistant at a reputable law firm, and his other sister, Diane, even with all her shortcomings, was a manger for a national bank branch. Both of his brothers, upon graduating high school, had jumped ship and enlisted in the army. They were only heard from on holidays, but Eddie knew they were doing something with their lives. Here he was, a soldier boy for a conniving drug dealer and working at a job where he checked levels of shit in the water all night. He was making chump change and was a failure.

Eddie looked around at the young boys on the different corners throwing their lives away. "They don't have a damn clue." He said to no one in particular.

He sat in his car watching the activities for another hour before he was satisfied that everyone and everything was secure. If they messed up, his ass was on the line too. This was yet another reason that this job was only temporary. He couldn't be responsible for knuckleheads. Eddie glanced at his watch and put his car in gear. There was one more spot to check before he went to work at the plant. He looked at himself in the rearview mirror.

"Time to push off man." He sighed and drove off to his next destination.

*****

"Do you think he loves me?" Ayanna asked sadly.

She and Cedric were sitting on their grandmother's porch eating supper. Everyone else was scattered throughout the house eating and laughing.

"Who?"

"Eddie, of Course."

"Aww come on sis." Cedric gently nudged Ayanna on her arm. "You know pops loves you."

Ayanna shook her head. "I don't know. I just think that maybe he feels guilty about not being around me all this time." She looked at her brother. "I mean…he came around you." She said with a hint of resentment.

They were both silent; each immersed in their own thoughts, until Cedric grabbed his sister's hand.

"I love you lil' sis."

Ayanna pushed back the tears that had sprang up. She didn't like people to see that side of her. It was part of her tough girl persona. You could get pushed around too easily when you showed weakness. This was something that she had learned early on. She squeezed Cedric's hand in acknowledgment, knowing that he would understand why she couldn't respond in kind just yet.

"Pops isn't your regular pops. You know what I mean?"

Ayanna shook her head to let her brother know that she didn't.

Cedric continued. "What I mean to say is that Pops is all street. I heard he was the man back in the day. Maybe that's why he didn't come around. He didn't want you caught up in all that street stuff. You're a girl so dads are always protective more. I used to hear him and my mom arguing because she didn't want him bringing me around all that. He ended up not coming around for a long time. I was real mad at them both too because I didn't understand." Cedric stopped and popped the last piece of cornbread in his mouth. Ayanna waited patiently until he finished.

"But when he did come around, I was cool with it." Cedric continued. "No need being mad at him. He is who he is. Didn't you tell me you two had a good time at Captain George's?"

Ayanna smiled at the memory. "Yes, I did. I can't believe my mom let me go on my birthday. I never thought she'd let me go since it was Thanksgiving too but she was really cool about it."

"Well that's good sis. Give him a chance. That's all he wants, you know." Cedric got up and grabbed his empty plate. "Look, I'm about to go in here and get a couple slices of grandma's sweet potato pie and then get on the piano. You coming?

Ayanna waved him off. "No. you go ahead. I want to stay out here.

When her brother had gone inside, Ayanna thought back to their conversation. She really didn't like being angry with Eddie. She had thought that when she met him she would be happy and be able to show him off. She had been envious of her cousins and her friends' two parent homes. But her hopes had been shattered when she had seen how he lived and how he looked. He had eyes that couldn't be trusted. She knew eyes like that all too well. She was ashamed of him and refused to believe that she looked like him like everyone else always said. She would often look in the mirror and desperately look for features that resembled her mother's side.

"This is my granddaddy's nose."

"My eyes. That's definitely my mom."

"These lips come from my grandma Liz."

Ayanna had even tried to change her walk because people said she walked like Eddie too. She now covered her hairline, identical to her father's, with bangs. To Ayanna, he was a failure. But Cedric did have a point. Eddie seemed to be trying his best to prove himself worthy. She remembered when she first met him, and what she said about giving him a chance. She had wanted no part of him but her yearning for a real father had taken over her. If he hadn't mentioned the fact that she had a brother, she would have walked away and never returned. But here she was.

Ayanna stared off at her grandmother's lush flower garden. One could lose themselves in the beauty and smell of the many flowers. Appreciation for nature was something that she had inherited from her mother and Ayanna felt like she could soak in the content feeling forever. Among the century old trees that surrounded her grandfather's house, which housed birds singing sweet melodies, she could get away from the worries of her world. There she had imagined she was the daughter of a superstar father. She had lots of friends who always slept over at her mansion. Her father would buy her the best clothes and toys and they always took trips around the world. Her mother didn't have to work two jobs so she was always in a good mood and was never tired. All of her mother's time would be spent with her. But, of course, this was all just a dream.

Even though her reality was much different, Ayanna still yearned for her father's love, so she was going to open up more to him. She really did have a good time with Eddie on her birthday. Her mother had been really cool about it but she knew that her Lynette had been a little disappointed. Her birthday only fell on Thanksgiving once every few years and her mother loved celebrating both occasions at once. Ayanna was grateful she had been allowed to go. Andrew had grumbled about her leaving her "real" family but he was always grumbling about something. Lynette and Ayanna had paid him no mind at all.

Ayanna heard music coming from inside the house. She knew that Cedric was warming up and telling her to come inside to join him at the same time.

"At least I got a good deal on a big brother." She murmured to herself while hurrying inside to join him.

*****

The applause could still be heard in Rose's living room as everyone stood around Ayanna and Cedric who had just performed for the family.

"Chile, you got a beautiful voice. You got that from me you know?" Diane beamed at her niece.

"She's right you know." Rose spoke up. "Diane used to win all kinds of talent shows in school. I don't know why she didn't do something with it." Rose eyed her daughter who waved her away and smacked her teeth.

"And what about my handsome nephew?" Boomed the voice of Anthony, Evelyn's husband. "That young man can play as well as Ray Charles."

Cedric tried to hide his blushing cheeks. "I wouldn't say all that, Anthony, but I'm working on it." He elbowed his sister in the ribs. "We make a good team, huh?"

Ayanna folded her arms. "You alright, I guess. Even if I did do all the work." She teased.

"All the work? All you did was sing a few off-key lines." Cedric shot back.

Ayanna punched him in the shoulder. "If I was off key then it was because I was trying to find the tune you were pounding on the piano."

"Don't mess with my art, lil' sis." He put up his hands like he was choking her.

Diane started laughing. "You two are a trip."

Ayanna wasn't used to having this much love shown to her by so many people. Her maternal side of the family was a bit stricter. On her paternal side, everyone was "free to be me" and everyone was referred to on a first name basis. Even her grandmother told Ayanna to just call her Rose. Ayanna, because of her upbringing, just couldn't grasp the idea.

Ayanna didn't feel comfortable with that rule, so she was the only one who used the traditional aunt, uncle, and grandma when addressing her family. They would just smile and shake their head. Her Aunt Diane said she liked the way it sounded, though, and told her to never stop.

The rest of the day consisted of the men gathering around the television for Sunday football. The women were in the kitchen gossiping and cleaning up while the children listened to music in Mia's room. Ayanna was searching for some new tapes to listen to when she heard a familiar voice.

"Hey pretty girls. Whatcha doing up here?" Eddie danced his way into the room causing Mia, Kaley, and Nita to giggle. Ayanna continued searching for music not bothering to look up.

"Eddie, you know you can't dance." Kaley said looking at Eddie's footwork.

"Well let's see what you got." He challenged.

Kaley suddenly got shy. She laughed and ran behind Ayanna. She had clung to her older cousin from the day they first met. She always ran to her when she became nervous or embarrassed, knowing that Ayanna would be her 'hidden courage.'

Eddie shook his head and folded his arms. "See? Just what I thought. Somebody's chicken."

Ayanna spoke up. "She's not chicken. She just doesn't want to show you up." Kaley's head popped up from behind Ayanna and she shook her head up and down.

Eddie raised an eyebrow. "Is that so?"

"Yep." Was the curt reply.

"This girl is tough as damn nails." Eddie thought. "Well

I guess I'd better be headed back downstairs then." He eyed Ayanna. "I can't take the competition."

Mia rushed forward. "Don't go Eddie. You don't ever come around." She pointed to the rest of the girls. "We made up a routine and we can show it to you."

Ayanna gave her the evil eye. "It's not ready yet, Mia." She was nervous about performing for Eddie. "Didn't I just say that I was going to open up more?" She thought.

Eddie and her cousins were staring at her. Nita put her hand on her hip. "Yes, it is Ayanna." She snapped. "I wanna show Eddie too. Come on!" She sounded just like her mother.

Eddie cleared his throat uncomfortably. "Look, if you girls need to practice then I understand. I can come back."

"No we're ready, aren't we Yani?" Nita glared at her cousin.

Ayanna reluctantly agreed. Anita could be extremely pushy when she wanted to be.

They did their dance routine to Michael Jackson's Billy Jean and for that brief period, Ayanna lost herself in the fun time they were having together. Her father clapped loudly when they were done and Ayanna accepted his hug when he offered it.

They were wishing that tiny moment in time would last forever, but sadly, it wouldn't.

Tenth Chapter

"So you're going to keep seeing Marcus? You should."

Rita and Lynette were walking around Clover Leaf Mall. They had decided to have a girl's day out and Ayanna had been allowed to take her schoolmate Kenya along. Lynette had slipped Ayanna twenty-dollars and told both girls to meet them in front of the mall in two hours.

Lynette's eyes visibly brightened at the mention of Marcus. "Yeah. I guess I'll keep him around a little while longer." She joked.

"You guess? Child please. Every time I turn around, that man is doing something sweet for you and he ain't even local." Rita sucked her teeth. "I need to find somebody from out of town. You think he's got any friends that like a woman with a little extra...?" She looked down at herself. "Let's face it. A little extra everywhere."

"Rita, any man would be lucky to have you whether you're a size two or a size twenty-two. How many times do I have to tell you that?" Lynette asked, a little annoyed because she was tired of her friend putting herself down in subtle ways.

Rita smiled. "You're right, Netty. I know Clarence loves all this."

Lynette rolled her eyes. "I know one thing. If you do lose

any weight, you just make sure that you give it all to Clarence. Can you at least get the man up to a hundred pounds?" She almost choked, laughing at her own joke.

Rita stopped walking. "I told you about talking junk about my man. I thought we were talking about you and Marcus any damn way."

Lynette gave her a tight one-armed hug. "Come on here woman and stop being so sensitive. You know I'm just messing with you. Come on so we can do a little shopping, grab the girls, and get something to eat."

*****

"Ayanna, come and look at these earrings! Hurry up!" Kenya was eyeing a pair of small gold hoop earrings with tiny diamonds in the corner dangling down.

Ayanna hurried over. "What is it girl? I was looking at a cute pink top in the back.

"Just come here! Forget that top for a minute." Kenya said impatiently.

Ayanna looked at the price of the earrings after Kenya had shown them to her. "There's no way that you can get these. They cost fifty-dollars!"

Kenya gave Ayanna a sly smile. "They may be that much for the average person but not for me."

Ayanna was smart enough to know what her friend was up to but also smart enough to know not to get involved. She stepped back and looked around. "I'm not trying to get in trouble for you. You're on your own."

Kenya's eyes narrowed. "If I get caught then I'll just say that you helped me by being my lookout. People have already seen us hanging out together in this store."

Ayanna, who was more afraid of her mother possibly finding out about her being involved in a theft, than being caught by mall security, was not backing down. Her mother's wrath would be ten times worse. "Whatever. You're supposed to be my friend but I can see how it is now. Like I said; I'm out of here. My mama would kill me."

Kenya grabbed Ayanna's arm who snatched it back. "Look." Kenya whispered. "I'm just going to slip these in my pocket really quick and no one will ever know, see?" Kenya skillfully slipped the earrings in her inside coat pocket and started easing towards the entrance to the store.

"Well hey there young lady. You're Eddie's daughter, aren't you?"

Ayanna looked up, not far, to see the fattest man she had ever seen. She had no idea how he could possibly see out of his thick glasses. It must have been like looking out the bottom of mason jars.

"I'm sorry but I don't know you." She replied cautiously and backed up.

Sweetman grinned at this little suspicious carbon copy of his employee. When he had spotted her in the store, he had known instantly who she was. He could easily spot a thief and had known her friend was up to no good by the way she kept glancing around. His suspicions were confirmed when he had seen her slip the earrings in her coat. Amateur. But he couldn't help but wonder if she might grow up to be useful to him.

"Of course not. I'm sorry. I'm a good friend of your dad's. We go back a long time. He talks about you all the time." He lied.

"He does?"

"Don't look surprised. He told me how pretty and smart you are."

Sweetman didn't look like any friend that her father would have and Ayanna didn't believe him. She would ask Eddie later on about this stranger who hadn't given a name. "Okay, well, nice meeting you sir." She nudged Kenya towards the door, who had been looking around the entire time to find something else to steal.

"You know these are some really nice earrings. I bet you wish that you could have a pair." Sweetman was holding up the same pair of earrings Kenya has taken.

Ayanna looked nervously at the jewelry. "Uh...they're okay. I can't afford to get them, though."

"Well I'll tell you what. Since I'm such good friends with your dad, why don't I get you these as a gift? He told me you just had a birthday." Sweetman dangled the earrings in front of her.

Ayanna was astonished. Why was this stranger trying to buy her a gift? She was almost positive that he knew something he wasn't telling. "I don't think my mom would like that." She shook her head.

Sweetman looked at Kenya with a smirk. "Well your friend has a pair. It's only fair that you have a pair too, don't you think?"

Kenya folder her arms. "I don't know what you're talking about?" She said defensively.

Sweetman chuckled. "I bet your inside pocket would tell a different story. You want me to tell you which side they're on?"

Ayanna's eyes got big. "Are you going to tell on us?" Kenya wasn't saying anything, playing the tough girl role. She narrowed her eyes at Ayanna.

Sweetman tilted his head, coyly. "Now why would I do that? I told you that I was a friend of your dad." He pointed to Kenya. "I don't know about your friend, though. It sounded to me like she was a snitch. I don't take care for snitches."

Kenya had a sheepish grin on her face. "I wasn't going to tell nobody. I was just trying to get her to stop being so scared" She took out the earrings. "See, I'm even putting them back. Please don't tell on me, mister."

Sweetman stared at Kenya and scratched his chin. "I guess I can let you slide." He leaned closer to her. "Let's just say you'll owe me later on down the road, Okay?"

Kenya, not knowing the true meaning behind his statement, was relieved. "Thanks."

Sweetman turned to Ayanna. "You sure you don't want those earrings?"

"No thanks, but thanks again for not telling on us."

Ayanna and Kenya ran out of the store, more than ready for the ordeal to be over.

"No problem." Sweetman whispered, staring off in the girl's direction. "No problem at all."

*****

"You girls have a good time?"

Lynette and Ayanna were in the living room watching television. Ayanna was sitting on the floor between her mother's legs with half of her hair braided.

"Yes, mama, I had a good time today."

"Well, next time we have a girl's day out, you can invite your friend Kenya again." Lynette said as she parted Ayanna's thick hair.

Ayanna shook her head causing her mother to make a

crooked part. "I don't think so, Ma. I just want it to be me and you."

Lynette froze with the comb in mid-air. "You sure you don't want to take a friend? She asked puzzled.

Ayanna hesitated before answering. "Yes ma. I'm sure I just want it to be me and you."

Lynette turned her daughter around gently to face her. Something didn't seem right. She knew her child. "Is there something you're not telling me, Ayanna?" She asked in a concerned voice.

Ayanna started to tell her mother about Kenya almost taking the earrings and about the fat stranger who claimed to be her dad's friend and then tried to bribe her. She wanted to tell her mother a lot of things, but feared that she would worry or be upset. This time was no exception.

"Mama, don't look so worried. I would just rather we go together since you're always working." She contorted her lips into her best pout. "Can it be just us from now on?"

Lynette pulled her daughter in a tight embrace. "Oh baby, am I working too much? I only work the way I do because I want us to get our own place and make our own rules. You know? Have our own space." Lynette stroked her daughter's soft hair. "I also work hard, baby, so you can have the things you need and most of what you want. I will never let you go without me."

Ayanna shook her head in understanding as her mother gently released her. "I know mama."

Lynette looked at her daughter for a moment. She knew when Ayanna wasn't being truthful all of the way. Something else was bothering her and she was determined to find out what. "You know I can cut back my hours from Safeway since

I've been able to get Eddie to help out a little. We would be able to spend more time together at night instead of you being around your grumpy ole' granddaddy and uncle. Would you like that?"

Ayanna suddenly felt guilty because she knew how hard her mother worked for them. Some nights Lynette would come home so tired, she would fall out on her bed fully clothed; complete with shoes. Ayanna would tip-toe in and remove her mother's shoes when she would discover her in the room asleep. But, her mother said it was worth it because one day her hard work would pay off and they would have their freedom.

"Just the two of us." Lynette would always say.

And Ayanna believed her.

But, now she had inadvertently caused her mother to think that she wasn't taking good enough care of her by working too much. Sure, she wished her mother didn't spend so much time out as she did but she wanted to move out just as bad; if not more than her mother. Ayanna did her part by not asking for extra things even when she became envious of the flashy girls at school.

She also enjoyed spending time with Lynette on her days off. They would go to the movies, art museums, outdoor festivals in the park; you name it and they did it. She would often hear her aunts whisper about how Lynette was never around for her daughter and how unfit she was but Ayanna knew better and always defended her. There was no one else. Ayanna had nursed swollen lips several times when her aunts had forgotten she was around and when they downed her mother, she had quickly jumped to her defense. She refused to let her mother think that she felt the same way as the people who were supposed to love her.

Ayanna held her mother's gaze. "Mama, you don't have to give up your job or anything. We always do stuff together and have lots of fun. I just think I would have liked it better today if it was just you and me. Nothing's wrong, Ma. I promise." She wished she hadn't.

Lynette smiled. "Okay, baby, if you say so. Turn back around so I can finish doing this head of yours."

"I'll get to the bottom of this later."

Eleventh Chapter

Sweetman sat in his den behind his desk smoking a cigar. He had just finished going over his books and was pleased with his current finances. It was a compulsion of his to make sure that his money was in order every morning, and every night to make sure nothing was tampered with. He had been this way since he got his first job as a barber shop sweeper on the weekends when he was fifteen. He also helped his father sell whiskey in the back of their house in the woods, at the time. He would tally up every cent from both jobs when he took his cut just to save up for college.

He had grown up relatively poor in Dinwiddie County. His father worked for a lumber company that required maximum work for minimum wages. His father's hands still had sores on them, as a result of the grueling work he had done for so many years. As a young boy, Sweetman, hated to see his father come home every night broken and tired. He had vowed early on that he would be successful and pay his parents back for all of their hard work and endless love and support. They had recognized his drive and encouraged him to be better than them.

If his parents knew what he was doing after hours, they wouldn't be so proud. He had never told any of his family about his drug business. He trusted his family, outside of his parents, as much as he trusted his enemies. If they knew, his parents would surely find out and probably disown him while everyone else would have their hands out. That's how his family had always been. They all wanted something for nothing. He had been taught and shown differently in his household so he never associated much with either side of his family. He didn't want anyone to know that he came from a weak stock; people who were dimwitted and selfish. He had built his business from cleverness and determination and he would not let it be compromised.

Speaking of compromised....

Sweetman stared out of his bay window overlooking the street and continued puffing on his cigar. Eddie had come to him the other day wanting to get out of the drug game. He had looked like he was back to shooting heroine and had barely been able to get his words out, he had been shaking so badly. Of course, Sweetman had known this would happen. He had known Eddie since he had come to Richmond to attend Virginia Union University. Eddie had been a fast-talking cocky street hustler. He and his crew sold marijuana to the majority of the students at the school. Sweetman had admired their money-making skills but thought they were stupid for being so open about it. Never envying their prosperity, he simply watched and saw how the faithful potheads kept coming back for more and more. He never cared about any of their possessions.

Not until he saw her.

Sweetman had been walking across the campus when he spotted a leggy red-boned fox standing with Eddie's crew. She had on baby-blue hot pants and a white halter top. She had her medium length hair brushed back and flipped on the ends. To Sweetman, she was the most beautiful girl he had ever seen. Not being blessed with good looks, he knew he didn't stand a chance but couldn't help but wish she were his. She should have been with anyone else but the bastard that she was with now, whose shabby treatment of her Sweetman witnessed that day.

"Yo, what the hell are you doing?

Sweetman turned his head in the direction of the caller and saw Eddie stomping across the grass.

"Yo, I thought I told your ass to stay in the car. Why are you out here parading around in front of all these niggas?"

The fox smacked her lips. "What do you mean? You better watch who the hell you're talking to. I didn't feel like sitting in that hot ass car and these supposed to be your people. So what are you worried about? You can't trust them around me?" She folded her arms and rolled her eyes. Sweetman had to admire how the petite little fox had stood up to Eddie.

Eddie glared at her and then at his crew who were snickering at his expense. Suddenly, he drew back and before anyone could blink, he slapped her across the mouth drawing blood. "What the hell is so funny?" He yelled to his crew. "I don't hear you talking shit now!" He directed at his girl. "Now get in the car!"

The fox stared at Eddie holding her mouth with one hand and was balling and un-balling the other hand in a fist. Finally, she relented.

Sweetman would never forget that moment as he watched her sadly get in the car and stare straight ahead, embarrassed.

He would see her again from time to time walking with her friends or hanging on Eddie's arm. One time, he caught her eye and she gave him an adoring smile. It was the kind of smile that thanked him for noticing and appreciating her beauty. Then she was gone. He didn't see her anymore after that because he transferred to Howard University. But he never forgot her or Eddie's mistreatment of her.

He wasn't going to let Eddie go just yet. Sweetman despised men like him. On the outside waving their plumes around like a peacock but on the inside pure coward. He represented street thugs mimicking movies glorifying hustlers but having no real clue to reality. He was going to make him as miserable as he had made her that day. Sweetman knew nothing about her except that she was beautiful and for one fleeting moment, had smiled at him like no other woman had ever smiled at him before. He could not forget about her.

Sweetman turned back to the paper lying neatly on his desk. He would give Eddie more corners to oversee and watch him fold. He already had someone else in mind to take his place. Using the knowledge of his daughter's identity, Sweetman would play him like a fiddle.

It would be fun.

*****

Eddie lay his head back on his couch and let the incredible sensation engulf him. He didn't care that the feeling would only last for a few minutes, but he craved it; even fantasized about it. He untied his belt from around his arm just above the elbow and let his entire body go limp. He didn't want to think about Sweetman giving him more responsibility even though he had practically begged him to let him go. With the powerful drug running through his veins and intoxicating his mind, he didn't have to think about a pre-teen looking to him for answers. Here, with his mind cloudy, he didn't have to worry about the longtime job he was on the verge of losing because he was a junkie.

"That's what I am. There's no way around it."

Eddie had thought about killing himself, but in the end, was too scared to go through with it. He had forgotten that he didn't possess the bravery to carry out such a cowardly act. He had to get out of this deal with Sweetman. Eddie didn't care about the money anymore. He just didn't want to be part of the streets anymore. It was too dangerous and had changed too much since he had been a young thug. He had explained this to Sweetman who simply gave him a smug look and shot him down cold. He had told Eddie that he was too valuable and wanted him to continue working for him a little while longer. He had seen something in Sweetman's eyes that didn't settle right with him. Was it spite? Did he take joy in knowing that Eddie was less than happy under his leadership? Eddie pondered the thought for a moment before shaking it away. What had he ever done to Sweetman? Hadn't he been a loyal customer for years with never a bad word between them?

Then Sweetman had the nerve to mention Ayanna. He could still feel the chill when Sweetman had spoken to him as he was walking away dejected.

"Did I mention that you've got a beautiful little woman in the making?"

Eddie had stopped mid-stride. How the hell did he know what Ayanna looked like? The hairs stood up on the back of Eddie's neck. Was Sweetman threatening him?

He slowly turned around. "No you didn't." Eddie and Sweetman stared each other down. Big Mike shifted; hand ready to grab his gun if necessary.

Sweetman finally smiled, while Eddie continued to glare at him. "No need to get upset, my man. I'm merely giving you a compliment. I happened to run into her at the mall. It wasn't hard to see that she's yours. She looks just like you."

"This muthafucka don't know that I will kill him and suffer the consequences later over my damn daughter." Eddie thought. He didn't say anything; just continued to glare at Sweetman.

Sweetman continued. "I mean....I'm just saying..." He straightened up in his chair and took a puff of his signature cigar. "You wouldn't want something to happen to such a precious gift."

"What the fuck!" Eddie came rushing toward Sweetman but abruptly stopped short as he stared down the barrel of a 45mm gun. Big Mike's eyes were daring Eddie to move. "Man, why you got to be threatening my daughter? I have never did nothing for you to be shittin' on me the way you're doing now." Eddie's eyes were darting back and forth between Big Mike and Sweetman.

"On the contrary....." Sweetman eyed Eddie and didn't finish his sentence.

Eddie was left in the dark; wondering where he had gone wrong.

"Shit! Now my high is shot to hell!" Eddie grumbled as his eyes focused on his surroundings. He glanced at the clock on the wall. He had to do something but he had no idea what it was. He couldn't even remember how long he had been closed up in his room. Ever since his conversation with Sweetman, everything had been a blur. He knew, eventually, Sweetman would come for him but right now, none of that mattered.

"Damn, my mouth is dry." He got up and went into the kitchen. He couldn't find a clean cup anywhere. They were all piled up in the sink with dirty plates still caked with food. The dryness in his mouth overwhelming, Eddie turned on the faucet and stuck his face under the water gulping down as much as he could. When he was done, the bubbling in his stomach was unbearable and he promptly threw up in the kitchen sink. Exhausted, he shuffled back to his couch and dropped down heavily. He looked around for his supply of heroin and the materials he needed to get his high going again. Just a little. No need to overdo it.

"What was it I had to do? Damn. Oh well." He shrugged it off.

As his veins filled once more, Eddie forgot everything that didn't matter and, unfortunately, everything that did, as well.

Twelfth Chapter

"Are you serious? You really want me to come down to North Carolina and visit you? Now you know if I come then Ayanna's coming too? Oh, I'm so excited!" Lynette said, all in one breath as she gushed to Marcus on the phone.

Marcus laughed on the other end. After months of talking to Marcus, his laughter still felt like a cool summer breeze to Lynette. She was falling in love. Marcus came to see her every time his truck route took him through Richmond which was at least three times a month. Lynette looked forward to those occasions and was visibly happy every time he was in town.

"Gal, you hit the lottery and not sharing the money?" Andrew would grumble. "Damn shame since I raised you."

Lynette would just laugh and go about her business humming away. Even Ayanna knew that she could get away with extra when Marcus was coming in town.

They hadn't slept together. Lynette didn't want to rush it and lose out on having a good man. She had a good track record with men, except for one in particular, and she wanted to keep it that way. Marcus wined and dined her almost to the point of embarrassment. He constantly told her how beautiful and intelligent she was. They could hold each other captive with conversation for hours which was something that Lynette hadn't had in a very long time.

"Why are you laughing at me? I can't believe you're laughing at me." Lynette went into schoolgirl mode.

"I'm sorry. You just sound so cute when you're excited and it makes me feel good to hear that you're happy. And for the record, I wasn't talking about just you coming down anyway. Of course, I want Ayanna to come but the night is ours." Marcus lowered his voice as if telling her a secret. "I know I could make you extremely happy if you visit me at my home."

The sexual tension had been mounting between them for quite some time. More recently, she knew that if she went to his home, she would surrender to his touches and his kisses. He knew exactly what he was asking of her; knew that under the blanket of privacy and candlelight, she couldn't resist his advances. Still, she couldn't say no to his request.

"We'll cross that bridge when we get to it." Lynette said coyly. "Right now, I'm just happy you want me to come see you."

"Well what's it going to be?"

"Oh." Lynette shook her head from side to side. "Of course. I've got to look at my finances and..."

Marcus cut her off. "Don't worry about that. I wouldn't think of asking my lady to pay to come and see me."

"Did he just call me his lady?" "Well I appreciate that. Just give me a date so I can let my job know and put in for my vacation time."

They discussed their plans. Lynette had decided not to bring Ayanna simply because she didn't want her daughter to be uncomfortable. Ayanna had met Marcus twice and even though they had hit it off eventually, Lynette didn't want to push it. Ayanna had an uncanny way of pushing back.

She tended to be possessive of her mother at times. Lynette was going to drive down to North Carolina early on Friday morning and come back Sunday night. It was only a 4 ½ hour drive so Lynette would have plenty of quality time to spend with Marcus. He kept Lynette's ear glued to the phone with all of the things they were going to do when she arrived.

"Charlotte is a thriving city, growing by the day. I'm going to take you to all the best restaurants and jazz clubs. We're going to take a walk downtown at night and take in the night life. You'll love it, Lynette." Marcus could barely contain his enthusiasm.

They ended their call with "I miss you" and Lynette was still beaming.

A million thoughts were going through her head at once. What should she take with her? Who would keep Ayanna for her while she was away? She knew that she would have to hear everybody and their snide remarks about her leaving, but Lynette didn't care. Why should she always have to please everyone but herself? Marcus had brought back the fire in her and had made her realize how strong she was.

Jerome tried his best to avoid Lynette since that night he tried to choke her. It didn't seem as if he was angry. It was more like he was embarrassed or ashamed that he had done such a thing to his little sister. Andrew also stayed away from her more frequently. Lynette knew her father wished that he could have stuck up for her but he always had a weakness for Jerome. Lynette didn't care because she had grown accustomed through the years to her father cowering down to her older brother. She loved him and still brought him his favorite meal every Friday night which was Little Caesars cheese pizza with extra cheese.

Her family hindered her from doing the things she wanted to do. All she wanted to do was to spread her wings and fly. She just wanted to go for a little while and explore before she flew back to the nest to take care of her baby bird and teach her how to fly on her own.

Luckily, this life hadn't affected Ayanna. She had won several presidency awards for physical fitness and placed 2nd, due to a scoring miscount, two years in a row as the female representative for her school in several oratorical contests. Ayanna was a genius with words and impressed teachers at several schools with her speeches. Her daughter was becoming a young woman with a good head on her shoulders and a bright future. Just the other day, Lynette had caught a surprised Ayanna looking at her sprouting, unevenly matched breasts. She had to laugh at the confused expression on Ayanna's face as she stared at her young chest.

Lynette wanted Ayanna to like Marcus. Ayanna had met him when he had invited them to lunch with him when he was in town. Ayanna was aloof at first, but Marcus's fun and charismatic nature had won her over in no time. Still, one could never tell with Ayanna. She could be smiling at you but, if you knew her, you could see something much more underneath. Lynette sighed and stared out of the living room window. If her daughter wasn't happy with her choice, then she would have to let Marcus go. She couldn't be with someone that Ayanna wasn't comfortable with, and unfortunately, her daughter knew it.

"Well, I'm not telling her where I'm going. I don't feel like hearing her mouth." Lynette said aloud.

Now she just had to figure out who she could get to watch Ayanna. That was the real dilemma. Her sisters always had something critical to say about her mothering skills. One didn't even have children and one needed to check her own bad ass son. As far as her sister, Simone, was concerned, there was no way she was going to leave Ayanna with that family. Who knew what new "daddy" was in the kids' lives? Lynette didn't want her daughter exposed to all of that. There was no way she could leave her baby at home with her father and brother. Ayanna would need counseling for the rest of her life. She had cut herself off her from her friends since Michael's death. She didn't want to be reminded of that past life which she now started to realize had been selfish. The only person that Lynette could really think of was Diane. Ayanna always enjoyed spending time with Diane and Anita. Anita was bright and funny just like Ayanna and Lynette liked them spending time together.

Lynette smiled and turned away from the window. It was time to make that call so she could get down her road to happiness.

"Hey Lynette! What's going girl? How's my favorite niece doing?" Diane could never seem to maintain a soft tone."

"I'm doing fine and so is Ayanna. You know she won another 2nd place medal for her speech downtown. Did she tell you?" Lynette knew Ayanna usually shared all of her achievements with her aunt.

"No, I haven't seen my baby for a while. I've been busy with the church and my mama. Ayanna's been hanging out with Evelyn and the kids."

"Oh." Lynette was a little miffed at herself for not knowing where her child had been spending her time and laying her head. Maybe her family was right about her not being a good parent. Usually she would just drop Ayanna over at Eddie's and then go on about her business, quickly, so she could avoid seeing him.

"Lynette, you still there?" Diane huffed into the phone.

"Oh yeah. I'm still here. I just got distracted for a minute." Lynette had almost forgotten what she had originally called about. "Listen Diane. I wanted to ask a favor of you. See…"

Diane cut in, "Lynette, I'm sorry honey but I don't have any money. You know if I had it though…"

"No. No. Let me finish." Diane could really get on Lynette's nerves sometimes, but right now she needed her." I was going to say that I'm going out of town for a few days and I was wondering if Ayanna could stay with you. I'm not leaving for another two weeks."

"Out of town, huh?" Diane whispered as if someone were really eavesdropping. "What's going on out of town, girl?"

Lynette should have known that Diane was going to be nosey. "Nothing much girl. I'm just catching up with a friend."

"A friend? Well does your friend have a brother or a cousin or something? Washington is working my last nerve and I need to get away from his ass." Diane whispered loudly.

Lynette was growing impatient. Was this woman serious? "Sorry Diane. Someone else has beat you to punch and placed their order for a family member to be thrown their way. Besides, Diane, if you go with me, then you can't watch Ayanna for me. I'll ask my friend when I get there if there's someone worthy of you but I hadn't planned on taking anybody extra."

"I knew it! Who is he girl? Where are you going off to that you've got to be all secretive?" Diane shouted causing Lynette to take the phone away from her ear.

"Diane, calm down. I don't want all my business out there and you know how you can be."

"What you mean?" Diane didn't appreciate being called out.

"You know exactly what I mean. Remember that time I caught Vanessa with Frank in the back of her daddy's Impala and I told you in secrecy?" No reply. Just dead silence on the other end. "Uh huh. You went and told mouth-of-the-south Louise and she told everybody. Then, remember, it got back to Vanessa's boyfriend and he put her ass in the hospital and he spent six months in jail. I could've killed you. No one's seen Frank since."

"Oh yeah, I forgot about that. It was so juicy, I couldn't hold it in and I should have known I couldn't trust can't-hold-water-in-the-rain-with-a-bucket Louise. I felt really bad about Vanessa getting beat up like that." Diane said remorsefully. "But, this is a different time for me and I'm not going to tell anybody, Lynette."

She sounded so pitiful at the moment that Lynette decided she would let her in on her secret rendezvous knowing full well she would regret telling Diane later. "Okay girl, I've been seeing someone a lot who lives in North Carolina. I met him when he came through my line at Safeway. He's a truck driver, girl, and handsome as hell too. I really like this one. He treats me like gold." Lynette couldn't hide the happiness in her voice.

Diane had to admit to herself that she was a little jealous. "Well it sounds like you might want to keep this one around, Lynette. How does he feel about my niece? Better yet, how's she feel about him? I don't want no mess because I will hurt a nigga over her."

"Don't get crazy, Diane. He likes her and she likes him too

but she won't admit it. And trust me, if there was a problem between them, that nigga would be gone from my life. You should know that from me dealing with your trifling brother."

"Yeah, I guess you're right but that's not a memory lane I think you want to go down right now." Diane changed the subject. "So when are you leaving and coming back?"

"Friday after next until Sunday evening. I want to get back in time to get Ayanna ready for school. I wanted to leave early on Friday morning when I send her off to school but then I won't have anybody to pick her up." Lynette scratched her scalp.

"Oh girl, I'll do it. Just give me the number where you're going to be and make sure that Ayanna's stuff is all packed. I can pick her up after school and we'll drop by and pick up her overnight bag. Go get yourself some, girl, and live a little."

Lynette chuckled. "Thanks girl. I really appreciate this. Ayanna loves coming over there."

"We love her coming over here too. Call me."

Everything was set.

Thirteenth Chapter

"Where'd your mom go, anyway? My mom just told me last night that you were spending the weekend here. She said she wanted to surprise me" Ayanna and Anita were in the living room flipping through magazines. Lynette had left earlier that morning, headed for Charlotte.

Ayanna shrugged her shoulders. "Who knows? I'd rather be over here anyway."

Anita looked at her cousin sadly. "They're still giving you a hard time over at your house? Why don't you and your mama just move away? I don't get it."

Ayanna turned the page of the magazine that she was reading so fast that it ripped. "It's not that simple, Nita, Okay? My mom is saving so we can get our own place."

"Alright, don't get so grumpy. You should ask Eddie to help, you know. He is your daddy."

Ayanna ripped another page.

"Hey! You're messing up my Word Up magazine. I want to put up my LL Cool J poster." She snatched the magazine away from her cousin and held it to her chest.

Ayanna ignored Anita. "I can't ask Eddie. Have you seen how he lives? He barely has enough to take care of himself.

Why did my mama have to pick him? I wish she would have picked someone like Marcus."

"Marcus?"

"Yeah. The guy my mama's seeing. He's real cool but of course I can't tell my mom that. She might think that it's okay to spend a lot of time with him or invite him out with us. He's temporary anyway. They always are." She mumbled the last part.

Anita's eyes beamed wide. "Your mom's got that many boyfriends?"

Ayanna shook her head. "No, not really." She reached for another magazine but changed her mind. "Anyway, I don't want to talk about this anymore. Why don't we go down to Reggie's house and see if he's home. Then we can grab the rest of the gang and hang out at the basketball court."

Anita wrinkled her nose. "Smelly Reggie? You know he has a crush on you. He was stupid enough to tell Cedric and your brother threatened to run him over with his bike if he came near you."

Both of the girls burst of laughing at the same time.

"Are you serious?" Ayanna managed to choke out. "Cedric really threatened him?"

"Yep. So let's skip Reggie and go straight for the rest of the gang. He'll probably show up anyway and stare at you from a distance." Anita said as she started giggling.

Ayanna hit her over the head with a pillow. "Let's go. My mom's not the only one who's going to have some fun this weekend."

*****

Lynette couldn't get over how much fun she was having in this quaint city. It had been an easy drive; a straight shot from Interstate 95 to Interstate 85 directly into Charlotte. There was good food, good people, and they even had their own basketball team, Charlotte Hornets. Marcus had met her off of the Graham Street exit and from there, they drove back onto to the highway and she had followed him home. Lynette was apprehensive at first when she had seen nothing but rows of shabby houses and liquor stores where they had met. But she soon relaxed when she saw that the area was getting better and better and the houses bigger and bigger. They finally came to a beautiful brick split-level home with a two-car garage. The yard was perfectly groomed with rows of various colorful flowers lining the house. Lynette felt like she had struck gold.

Marcus had shown her around his home which looked like it came straight out of Better Homes and Gardens. Both of his daughters' rooms were set up with princess themes. His room was all bachelor with black satin sheets on the bed which had red and black satin pillows on it. It looked to be about twenty fluffy pillows on the bed. He had mahogany furniture in his room. He also had a huge black bear rug on the floor that Lynette hoped was fake. She had been meaning to ask him about it.

It was Saturday afternoon and she was sitting on the back patio watching Marcus grill steaks and make a clambake. He was a renaissance man to Lynette. He could decorate, cook, clean, work on cars... you name it, and he could more than likely be able to do it. Lynette wasn't sure about his bedroom skills, though. Marcus had been content to make her as comfortable as possible and had not made any advances toward her. Lynette had to chuckle as she glanced over at Marcus She had heard him taking a shower at two a.m.; no doubt a cold one. Today she would meet his two daughters and Lynette couldn't help but be a little nervous. She knew how her own daughter could be and she didn't want the girls to think she was trying to take their mother's place. They had spent the night over at their friends' house the previous night so Marcus wanted to break the ice by throwing a barbecue.

The smell from the food was so tantalizing that Lynette's mouth had started watering. "Hey you!" Lynette shouted. "How much longer you going to keep the queen waiting, huh?"

Marcus smiled and made a low bow. "It will only be a moment, your majesty." He stood and did a quick analysis of Lynette's body. The woman was truly gorgeous. "Maybe I could get something done if you stop distracting me with those pretty brown eyes."

"Don't start no mess, Marcus." She glanced at her watch. "What time are Sinai and Ciara going to be coming home?"

Marcus flipped a steak. "Stop worrying. They'll be here soon enough and they're going to love you. That's why I sent them away last night. I wanted you to get settled and feel okay at my home before you met my girls."

Lynette settled back and continued to watch Marcus as she thought about what was waiting for her back home. Not much because all she really needed was Ayanna. She could see them moving to Charlotte and making a new life here. It wasn't that far from Richmond so they could visit as often as they wanted. Marcus had been selling her on the idea for months, after learning how her home life really was. He had listened attentively as she poured her heart out about dealing with her mother's death and her father drowning himself in alcohol to ease his grief and guilt of being left behind. Marcus held her close when she cried over her brother's abuse and how she longed for his love again. He even agreed with her when she spoke out against her sisters' controlling ways and the fact that she shouldn't be afraid of them. Lynette's mother has been the last person she had been able to be open with.

Marcus hadn't been pushy in his approach. He simply pointed out the advantages of starting fresh in a growing city that had so much to offer to her and her daughter. To Lynette, sometimes her family could be like shackles and there wasn't an ax or any batter in sight to get them off.

Marcus snapped Lynette back to reality when she heard him yelling at her. "Hey woman! You alright up there? My babies just pulled up so I'm going around front to get them and bring them back here to meet you."

All Lynette could do was smile and nod. All of a sudden, she felt like her shorts were too short and her hair wasn't right.

"Daddy, I told you that there aren't going to be very many people there. Taisha just wanted to have a little get together."

"And I told you Ciara that if there's no parents then there's no party. Now don't ask me again until Taisha meets that requirement. What is that child's mama thinking anyway?"

Lynette was getting more and more nervous with each passing moment. "Great. Now I've got to meet one daughter for the first time when she's mad at the world. She's going to hate me." Lynette tried to pull her shorts down to cover more leg. She could hear them getting closer. She started messing with her hair.

Marcus and the girls rounded the corner. "There she is girls. Say hello."

Lynette had been so busy playing with her hair, she hadn't noticed them advancing on her.

"Hello." They said in unison. Lynette couldn't get over how much they looked like their father.

"It's so nice to meet you both. Your father brags about you all the time." She pointed to the oldest and then the youngest. "You must be Sinai and you must be Ciara."

Sinai grinned at Lynette. "Thanks for pronouncing my name correctly. Most people don't get it right on the first try."

"You're welcome. I'm big on names and yours is too pretty to mess up." She turned to Ciara. "Your dad said that you could skate like a pro. Maybe we could go out to the rink and you can show me some things."

Ciara cut her eyes at her father. "I don't know if my dad will let me go. He might not think there are enough parents around."

Marcus pointed to the grill. "Get your behind over there and finish those steaks before you make me embarrass you. Don't think that I won't just because company's around."

Ciara started pouting. "But daddy....."

"What did I just say?" Marcus's voice boomed, making Lynette jump. Ciara hurried off toward the grill followed by her older sister.

"I've got her, dad." Sinai assured him.

"You better." Marcus huffed and turned back to Lynette. "Sorry about that. Ciara can be a handful."

Lynette wrapped her arms around him. "Don't worry. I know how it is."

The day ended up going very well. Ciara got over her teenage issues after Marcus threatened her and then the girls started focusing on Marcus and Lynette's relationship. They wanted to know everything. Where did they meet? How long had they been going out? What was her daughter like? Did she really like their dad or was she after any money (this came from Ciara who had to duck to avoid getting popped in the mouth by Marcus)? The list went on and on but Lynette didn't mind and she was very honest. They were anxious to meet Ayanna and were a little put off that she hadn't visited too. Lynette explained that the next visit would definitely include Ayanna.

Later, they went skating and sure enough, Ciara was the best out there. While Lynette teetered around the rink, Ciara would literally skate circles around her and laugh. She would skate backwards and grab Lynette's hands to pull her along. Occasionally, Lynette would catch Marcus staring at her with a smile on his face while he skated with Sinai. Sinai wasn't as good as her sister but she wasted no time showing off her skills as well.

By the end of the night, Lynette was so sore that she didn't think she would be able to sit down for at least a month. She had fallen no less than sixty times by her count but Marcus and the girls guessed somewhere neared to two-hundred.

"You guys wore me out tonight." Said an exhausted Lynette as they rode back to the house. When there was no answer, Lynette glanced in the back seat and discovered that both girls had fallen asleep. "Hmmm. I guess I'm not the only one who got worn out." She chuckled to herself and lay her head back on the headrest and closed her eyes. She was unaware that Marcus was silently praying that Lynette wasn't completely worn out because he still had some plans of his own for the night. Once they arrived at the house and the girls had gone to bed after hugging Lynette and saying goodnight, Marcus ran Lynette a hot bubble bath to help soothe her sore muscles. This was another new experience for Lynette who couldn't get enough. Marcus then gave her an out of this world massage with scented oils. Lynette had no shame as she allowed him to knead her naked body with his strong but gentle hands.

"How are you feeling?" Marcus asked in a husky voice.

"Words cannot describe how wonderful your hands feel." Lynette sighed.

This was all Marcus needed to hear as he bent down and kissed the small of Lynette's back. She let out a soft moan. "I want to make you feel like a woman should feel, Lynette." Marcus said between kisses. "Will you let me?"

Lynette was ready to let him do just about anything he wanted to do at this point. "I definitely won't stop you, if that's what you're asking."

Marcus lifted her hair off her neck and gently kissed her again. "Good. Prepare yourself then."

He then proceeded to truly introduce her to womanhood.

Fourteenth Chapter

"Gal, how are you going to pack up and move with a child where there's nothing but strangers? That just don't make no damn sense to me." Andrew was in the tool shed looking for his hammer. When he found it, he turned around to look at Lynette as if he was ready to hit her over the head with it.

"Daddy, I didn't say I was moving for sure. I just said I was thinking about it. Besides, people move away all the time for different reasons. I could get a better job with better benefits if I move to North Carolina."

"Gal you are talking nonsense. You can get a job right here in good ole Virginia."

Lynette closed her eyes and took deep breaths while she mentally counted to ten. No one understood how important this was to her and how much it would benefit Ayanna. They were all too blind or selfish to see. Ever since she had met Marcus two months earlier, she had been given the support and that extra push to be stronger and more determined to move away. She wanted Ayanna to be given every opportunity there was without having to hear criticism from her family. If Lynette stayed in Richmond, they would still try to have some type of control.

"Look daddy. I started out not wanting to tell you, but I

changed my mind out of respect. You know that I and Jerome don't get along and you also know I've been wanting to move for a while to be on my own. I haven't made up my mind yet but I will let you know when I do."

Andrew turned his back and started pretending he was searching for more tools and said nothing.

"Daddy, don't be like that." Lynette whined.

"I should have known this would happen. You get old and your children go off and abandon you like an old beat up car." Andrew mumbled.

"Daddy, I can't talk to you when you're like this." Lynette threw up her hands and stalked off towards the house. Andrew followed her.

"You know your sisters aren't going let you go without filling your ears up first. Lil' gal don't need to be uprooted from her family. This here is her home as much as it is yours where her blood is. If you go, then go by your damn self and leave my grandbaby here with me." Andrew huffed.

Lynette laughed so hard that tears formed in her eyes. Andrew stood by with an angry expression.

"What the hell are you laughing at?" He demanded.

Lynette finally composed herself. "Have you been drinking? I would never leave Ayanna here and go off somewhere by myself on a permanent basis. Are you serious? So you and everybody can talk about me like a dog and brainwash my child against me? Never. Jerome is abusive and all you do is feel sorry for yourself and drink all damn day and I'm sick of it." Lynette's chest heaved up and down as she released her anger. She had never disrespected her father before but she felt like she was at the end of her rope.

Andrew's shoulders sagged a little and he looked in his

daughter's eyes and saw the same fire in them that had been in her mother's. He knew that he hadn't made it easy on Lynette since his wife's passing. His grief had consumed him and he had expected Lynette to take away the pain of Liz's death to some extent. It was time to let her go and make a life for herself.

He waived Lynette away. "Hell, if it's that bad around here then take lil' gal and go on about your business." He finally replied, in a wounded voice.

"Like I said, I don't know if I'm going yet."

"Could've fooled me." Andrew glanced one more time at his daughter's determined expression and walked back to the tool shed swinging his hammer.

*****

Lynette was in the den playing Clue with Ayanna when she heard someone pounding on the back door.

"Mama, should I get the stick?" Ayanna said as she started to rise.

"No baby, I've got it. Just stay right here." Lynette got up and crept to the kitchen window and peeked out. There was Lynda standing on the back porch with her hands on her hips.

"Lynette, are you in there?" She pounded on the door again.

Lynette didn't feel like dealing with Lynda today. She and Ayanna had been spending all day together baking cookies and playing their favorite board games. But, if she didn't answer the door, her sister would just come back or worse; never leave. Lynette finally opened the door and greeted her sister.

"Hey Lynda. What brings you by?"

"You ain't taking my niece no damn where!" Lynda pushed Lynette aside and invited herself inside.

"What are you talking about, Lynda?" Lynette played dumb. "Damn. It hasn't been twenty-four hours since I told the old man I was thinking of moving and the drama's already started."

"You know what the hell I'm talking about. I talked to daddy this morning and he told me some mess about you packing up and taking Ayanna to South Carolina some damn where."

Lynette cleared her throat and tried her best to remain calm and not come out of the bag on her sister for coming at her the wrong way. "It's North Carolina and I told daddy more than once that I haven't made up my mind yet." She folded her arms in front of her. "What does this have to do with you anyway?"

"It has a lot to do with me if you're moving my niece away." Lynda wasn't going down without a fight.

Lynette shook her head. "You know…? I don't know why we're even having this conversation. If it was Simone moving, would you have a fit?" She threw up her hands in frustration. "You know what? I'm not talking about this anymore with you. Ayanna is my child."

"You're following some man, aren't you?" Was the quick response.

"Typical that you would say that." Lynette was fuming. "As a matter of fact, I happen to be seeing someone who lives there but he's not the reason that I'm thinking of moving; not the only reason, that is."

Lynda snorted. "Yeah right. I wasn't born yesterday. You're dragging that child down to God knows where so that your needs can be satisfied by someone who probably won't be around but for a few months."

Lynette had had it, "Does anyone ever listen?" She screamed. "You know what? I'm done thinking about it. Ayanna and I will discuss this ourselves and what we do doesn't have to impact you and the rest of the clan one bit."

"Mama, what's going on? What do you want to talk to me about?" Ayanna had entered the kitchen without her mother and aunt realizing it.

"Ayanna, I've told you about butting into grown folk's business!" Lynette snapped.

"No! No!" Lynda wagged her finger in front of Lynette's face. "She's a part of this too. How come she doesn't need to know that her mom is about to rip her away from her family and go off philandering with some damn man she barely knows?"

Lynette got in her sister's face. There was no trace of fear. "I can't believe you just said that shit to my daughter. Don't you ever disrespect me in front of her again or I'm going to show you just how much I've grown up."

Lynda blinked and didn't say anything from shock. Lynette never spoke to her like that.

Lynette turned to Ayanna. "I've got something I want to talk to you about. It's about us moving. Just let me speak to your aunt for a minute and then we can talk."

After Ayanna left, Lynette turned back to her sister. "Like I said; I'm done thinking about it and I'm damn sure not talking about it with you and the rest of my family." She waved Lynda off. "Now run back and tell that."

Lynda grabbed her purse and went to the door. As she opened it and stepped out, she turned around and looked at

Lynette. "You'll never make it alone. You'll come running back soon." She said coldly.

In response, Lynette simply smiled and closed the door in her sister's smug face.

*****

"So that's what you and Aunt Lynda were arguing about?"

Lynette and Ayanna had been talking for the past thirty minutes. Lynette had lain all her cards on the table leaving out nothing. She didn't want Ayanna getting secondhand information.

"Yeah baby. Everyone thinks that us moving is a mistake and you're going to be miserable. I didn't want you to find out like this."

"We wouldn't have to live with Mr. Marcus would we" Ayanna had a perplexed looked on her face.

"Of course not." Lynette embraced her daughter. "We would have our own place and live by our own rules. We could look forward to coming home instead of dreading it like we do now." She said referring to how the pair always became somber on the winding road back home after being away at a friend's having fun. "Hell, we could even bring company over for once without being embarrassed. I know you want your friends to be able to come over and sleep over sometimes. It would be great. All I have to do is put in a transfer at Safeway and wait for an opening which won't be long."

"Will I still get to see Cedric?" Ayanna whispered.

Lynette had forgotten about the bond that Ayanna and her brother had formed. She felt a wave of guilt which she quickly pushed aside. "Yes baby. We'll still be close enough where we can still visit pretty often."

Lynette released Ayanna and stared in her eyes. "Do you want to think about it? I'm not going to rush you into anything. I just want you to be happy."

"No Mama. I want to go. I don't need to think about it." Ayanna did her best to mask her fear of leaving the home where she had grown up. And what would her grandfather do without her around to protect him from her uncle and himself?

Lynette looked deep into her daughter's eyes knowing that there was something more there. She smiled down at Ayanna and embraced her as she rocked her. She was so proud of her.

First thing in the morning, Lynette put in a request for her transfer.

*****

Lynette and Ayanna jumped head first into making their big move. Both had their own reasons for being so excited. They had gotten over their fears (at least some of them) after discussing their plans. Ayanna was about to advance to the ninth grade and she figured she'd be meeting a whole new group of people anyway when she went to high school. So why not just meet them in another state? She would finally be able to be a teenager.

Lynette was excited about proving herself in a different environment. She planned on working hard when she went to North Carolina so that she could find a better job. Also, she secretly wanted to get Ayanna away from Eddie. She knew he was just setting Ayanna up for disappointment. He seemed nervous and shifty most of the time. Lynette was skeptical about letting her daughter visit him, but Ayanna insisted on giving him a chance. If she found out that he was using her again, then his relationship with Ayanna would be instantly terminated. Lynette had approached him once about it and he had vehemently denied it.

She planned on moving at the end of the school year which was four months away so she had to get her affairs in order quickly so her and Ayanna could travel to Charlotte. Apartments had to be found and Ayanna had to be registered for school.

Eddie was the only one who didn't protest to them leaving but Lynette hadn't expected him to put up much of a fight anyway. He didn't have a leg to stand on since he'd barely been in Ayanna's life since she was born. Lynette could have sworn, in fact, that when she told him about the impending move, she had seen a hint of joy in his face. Or had it been the light? It had gone away as quickly as it appeared and replaced by a look of rehearsed sorrow over Ayanna's leaving.

"Damn Lynette. We're just getting to know each other. You're taking her away already?"

"Whose fault is that? If you would have done right from the beginning then you would have known her a long time ago. Look," Lynette huffed. "I don't want to go back down memory lane with you. I suggest you squeeze in as much quality time as you possibly can. And don't act like you can't send for her during the summer or holidays. What about you visiting her? I fully expect you to keep helping take care of Ayanna too unless you want to end up in court too. I'm not playing with you this time around."

Eddie had lowered his head and rubbed his forehead. "Well I guess you got to do what you got to do."

Lynette had simply walked away.

She received calls daily from her brothers and sisters telling her how stupid she was to be "following some man" and dragging Ayanna with her. They just couldn't see that Marcus had only planted the seed in already fertile soil. It hurt Lynette dearly but she was determined to keep pressing forward and proving everyone wrong.

One Friday morning, she was enjoying the rhythm of doing simple house chores. Ayanna was at school, hopefully not getting into trouble and Andrew was at Mr. Carroll's store which would keep him occupied for hours. Lynette was humming to herself while folding towels when she heard a heavy knock at the back door. Usually, everyone from the neighborhood just called her name, opened the screen door, and came right in. Puzzled, she went to the back door only to find the entrance completely filled with a huge policeman. Behind him, Lynette could just make out a tall Caucasian woman with an ill-fitting tweed skirt and a cheap blouse that clung too tightly. Right beside her was Jerome with his lip slightly curled up on one side. Lynette's heart sank.

"What has he done?" Lynette grimly thought.

Even though she was at least a foot shorter than the policeman, she looked him square in the eye. "Yes. Can I help you officer?"

The giant in the doorway cleared his throat. "Are you, by chance, Ms. Lynette Beatrice Lee?"

Lynette's bowels began to move but she kept her face as calm as possible. She stepped out on the porch. "Yes. That's me officer. Again, can I help you?"

The policeman looked back at the woman behind him

who, as if on cue, stepped forward and gave a fake smile. "Yes mam. My name is Olivia Reynolds. I am a social worker who represents the Richmond Child Welfare and Protective Service. We received a call that there was negligence concerning a minor living here and we came to remove... ..."

Lynette raised her hand up in front of the social worker's face and cut her off. "What the hell do you mean negligence? I take damn good care of my daughter. Who the hell called you with this nonsense?"

Olivia shook her head. "I'm not at liberty to say, Ms. Lee, but I have to inform you that because accusations were brought against you for negligence and abuse we have to remove the child from the home until a formal investigation can be completed."

Lynette thought she was going to faint. How could someone do this to her? Abuse? This didn't make any sense. She looked up at her brother who was still standing behind the policeman smirking. Suddenly, she lunged at him. "You! You did this you son-of-a-bitch! Just couldn't stand to see us happy, huh?"

The policeman grabbed her by the waist before she could make it to Jerome.

He had jumped back surprised and was now looking back at Lynette with hatred. "You're a good-for-nothing so-called mother. That's what you are. You can run after whoever you want but Ayanna stays here."

Lynette couldn't believe what she was hearing. "This is a new low! How is lying on me going to help Ayanna?" She turned to Olivia. "Whatever my brother told you was a lie. He's making this all up because he doesn't want me to take my daughter away from all this bullshit. Please don't take my daughter away. It would kill me!"

"Ms. Lee, you have to calm down. I'm sure that everything will work out but, again, until we are positive that there is no abuse going on concerning the child, we have to remove her from the home. She will remain in a child welfare facility reserved for foster children until the inquiry is complete. If all goes well, and again I'm sure it will, your daughter should be back in your care within a week. Is she currently at school?" Olivia motioned for the policeman to release Lynette.

She jerked away. "Of course, she's in school. Where else would she be this time of day? Or did my brother tell you I force her to stay home and not go to school too? This is bullshit and hell no you can't have my daughter!"

Before anyone could blink, Lynette pushed Olivia out of the way and jumped on Jerome; hands around his throat. Jerome, being caught off guard, stumbled and fell backwards into the gravel with his sister's hands still around his windpipe. "You evil motherfucker! I can't believe you pulled this shit!"

The policeman quickly grabbed Lynette and pulled her off Jerome. "Mam, you cannot put your hands on him!" He shouted.

Jerome, who was picking himself off the ground and rubbing his neck sputtered, "Arrest her officer! She assaulted me and I want her out of here!"

"Arrest me? You're such a coward. Go ahead and do what you got to do. I'm gonna get your ass!" Lynette hissed at Jerome.

The policeman, still holding Lynette, asked Jerome. "Sir, are you sure you want to press charges against her for assault?"

"Hell yeah I want to press charges! Get her outta here officer!" Jerome screamed.

Olivia, visibly shaken and straightening her glasses shook her finger at Lynette. "Ms. Lee, I must say that this doesn't reflect favorably on your behalf. This will have to go in my report."

Lynette was crying uncontrollably and didn't have the strength to respond. All she could see was her and Ayanna's plan for a good future going up in smoke. "I know Jerome wasn't the only one who had to do something with this. I know it!" She thought grimly. She allowed the policeman to put her in the back of the squad car without putting up a fight.

Before the door was shut, Olivia leaned down to speak to Lynette. "Ms. Lee, we will make sure that your daughter is properly taken care of until this ordeal is over. She will be picked up at home after school and remain in the State's custody until further notice. We will keep you informed of the proceedings at all times." Olivia then gently touched Lynette's arm. "I am truly sorry about all of this. Please do your best to comply with everything that we ask and your daughter will be back with you in no time."

Lynette stared ahead and remained silent. Olivia sighed and closed the door and told the policeman that it was okay for him to leave. As Lynette was being driven away, she turned around and saw Jerome waving goodbye with a grin on his face.

*****

"Lynette Lee, you're free leave. You made bail."

Lynette, who had been curled up in a ball on the corner of the bench, opened her eyes. She had cried and screamed for hours until her throat was sore and she was too tired to move another muscle. Since she was arrested on Friday afternoon, she had been forced to stay in jail for the entire weekend asleep on her cot. It took her a moment for her to register where she was. "Who in the world would have bailed me out?"

The bars rattled open and she slowly walked through towards the awaiting female officer. She winced as the bars clanked loudly behind her as they were closed.

"Put a move on it miss so we can go ahead and get you processed out of here. I've got more people who need to take your spot." The officer gently tugged Lynette's arm who nearly tripped.

"What's the matter honey? Aren't you glad to be getting out of here" The officer shook her head and kept pulling Lynette along.

Lynette looked down on the floor. "I'm just tired. That's all." She doubted the officer even knew what she really meant.

She went through the motions of being processed to go home and was just about to ask who paid her bail when she heard a sad voice behind her.

"Hey sis. You alright?"

Lynette turned around to see Rita standing with a scarf around her head and smudged makeup. She looked like she had seen better days but Lynette felt nothing but relief at seeing her best friend. She hugged Rita as tight as she could. "You know how glad I am to see you right now. Shit went down at the house. Jerome has lost his damn mind! He got my baby taken away!" She couldn't hold back a fresh wave of tears. She had to get her daughter back.

Rita stared past Lynette. "I know what happened already." She said sadly. "I was at Lynda's when Jerome called."

Lynette stood up straighter and glared at her, "Well what the hell did they say?"

Rita looked down and paused for a moment. "The plan was to prove you an unfit mother and then get custody of Ayanna. You would have been free to go wherever you want after they forced you to sign away your rights."

Lynette shook her head. "You're not making any sense, Rita. Who did this to me?"

Rita finally looked her friend in the eyes. "Sis, I'm sorry but Lynda and your daddy set the whole thing up."

*****

"There's no way I'm staying here and if they think I am then they're crazy." Ayanna thought as she used a butter knife she had stolen from the kitchen to scrape at the paint that sealed the windows shut. She had been scraping for thirty minutes in an attempt to get through the decades of the painted and repainted window seal. She wasn't used to being confined and especially away from her family. She was angry and confused which only fueled her determination to escape from this cold place. No one would tell her anything, no matter how much she begged and pleaded. Everyone just kept telling her that she was here for her own safety. Safety? What were they talking about? Did they find out about her uncle and mom's fight in the kitchen? Oh no! Did they know she cut her uncle with a knife? She had to make sure they knew it was an accident. She thought back to the events that landed her in a state facility.

She had just gotten off the school bus with Kevin Daley's taunts behind her. "See you later chicken legs!"

She turned around and yelled, "At least I don't look like an Oompa-Loompa from the Chocolate Factory!" and ran off. She could hear the kids on the bus laughing. Before she ran around the house to get to the back door, she glanced over at the massive Weeping Willow just as a breeze swept through and the leaves swayed side to side. "Well hello to you too." She planned on conquering a few more branches today in an effort to finally make it to the top. But she never got the chance because when she made it into the house, her world turned upside down.

"Well hello. You must be Ayanna. I'm Ms. Olivia Reynolds."

Ayanna stopped in her tracks and blinked. Who was this funny looking white woman? The middle button on her shirt looked like it would pop any minute now. "Hi." She looked around. "Where's my mama?"

Before Olivia could speak, Jerome came around the corner and stood in the doorway. "Don't worry about where your mama's at. She ain't here like usual."

Olivia took off her glasses and rubbed the bridge of her nose. "Mr. Lee would you kindly step out of the room for a moment while I speak to Ayanna?"

Jerome looked at Ayanna and huffed. "Go right ahead. She's all yours." He proceeded to stomp out of the room.

Olivia leaned forward and gently spoke to Ayanna. "I'm sure you're wondering why I'm here."

Ayanna shook her head.

"Yes, well..." Olivia cleared her throat. "Your mother has been taken away due to an altercation with your uncle and..."

"What do you mean she's been taken away? He's the one with the temper! I want to see my mama!" Ayanna screamed.

"Young lady, calm down. I was a witness and your mother was extremely upset."

Ayanna wouldn't believe it. "Why was she upset?"

Olivia cleared her throat again. "Well, that brings us to the reason for my visit. There was a report of improper behavior here in the home so, by law, we have to remove you from the home until we get this matter resolved."

Ayanna's fist clenched. "I'm not going anywhere! Where's my mama?"

Jerome appeared again. "I told you she was stubborn. You'd better call somebody to help you with this one because it's not going to be me."

And the authorities had been called because Ayanna had refused to leave without knowing what was going on and where her mother was. They had to physically remove her much to the dismay of a frazzled Olivia who at that moment was reconsidering quitting drinking.

"Where are my aunts and uncles? How come nobody's come for me yet?" Ayanna thought.

She had been away from home for two days and it had felt like two years. Well if she could help it, she wouldn't be in this place for another day. She would leave them a note and let them know the truth about the knife incident with her uncle. She gripped the butter knife tighter and continued scraping.

Fifteenth Chapter

Sweetman was parked in the gravel driveway behind the dilapidated houses in Churchill. How anyone could live in these places was beyond him. At least it didn't look as bad at night. He was fixated on one house in particular at the end of the driveway whose current resident wasn't there at the moment. He was growing weary of stringing Eddie along and making him suffer. Every time he saw Eddie, there were more signs of him shooting up. His face was scarred and blistered, constantly nodding off, and moods changed from cold to hot in the blink of an eye. Sweetman knew the signs; had been around it for too long, and Eddie was beginning to cost him money. It was just a matter of time before Eddie would be removed from his duties permanently.

There was a soft tap at the window. Sweetman lowered the window. "Did you get it done?"

"Yes Sir. I did. Put it right where you told me to put it. He won't miss it."

Sweetman nodded. "Good. Good."

"I hope that bitch that be over there gets what's coming to her too."

Sweetman jerked his head towards the voice. "What bitch?"

"This high yellow woman that be dropping her lil' girl off sometimes. All I did was try to give her a compliment. Woman cussed me out!" The voice lowered and then chuckled. "That lil' girl was mighty pretty though. I could make a woman out of her real quick."

Sweetman stared ahead again. "You say everything's in place? In and out with no prints behind?"

"Yes sir. I was real careful."

"Good."

Ben never knew what hit him as he hit the gravel with a .44 caliber-sized hole in the center of his head.

*****

"I've got to leave that shit alone." Eddie thought as he staggered up to his street. He hadn't been home in three days. Instead, Eddie had chosen to drown his sorrows in drugs and prostitutes. For the past few days no woman had been too unattractive, body odor had been of no concern, and food had been unnecessary. He didn't even know if he had a job anymore. His supervisor had long ago told him that he was skating on thin ice and to start coming to work on time and actually work. He had called three days earlier and had feigned sick. It wasn't that far off the truth. He was sick. His supervisor had demanded a note from his doctor when he came back to work or don't come back at all, so Eddie was prepared to be jobless. Jobless meant less money and less money meant he couldn't get high as much as he wanted to. "Damn! What am I going to do now?" He wasn't getting the money he used to get from Sweetman. He had been told that business wasn't doing as well as it used to. Sweetman had said this smiling and sitting behind his desk with his massive body guard beside him. Big Mike had looked at Eddie as if he was daring him to jump. Eddie despised him. He knew Sweetman wasn't stupid. It was getting harder and harder to act like he wasn't using drugs any longer. No amount of brushing his hair or straightening out his clothes could cover up that fact.

As he got closer to his block, he spotted police cars flashing their blue lights. There must have been five or six cars, Eddie couldn't tell which, and they were all scattered along his driveway down from his house. Police tape was meticulously put up and several police officers were standing in front talking. Eddie tried to slip past them to get into his house.

"Hey Hey! You can't cross of this tape. We've got a crime scene here. Can't you see?" The policeman walked up to Eddie and stated.

Eddie stepped back a few feet. "I don't mean no harm officer. I live here." His eyes darted everywhere trying to find a way out.

The policeman raised his eyebrow. "You live where?"

Eddie pointed to the rundown house just beyond the police tape. "I live in that house right over there. I haven't done nothing wrong officer. I just want to go home." Eddie threw up his hands.

The police officer looked from Eddie to the house and then gestured for his partner to come over. "This guy here says he lives in this house?" He pointed.

His partner looked Eddie up and down. "Yeah I believe it. You get a lot of squatters staying in these boarded up houses."

Eddie shook his head. "No officer. I'm not squattin'. I pay to live here; been here for a few years now." The instant the words came out, he was embarrassed.

"Well what do you know about what happened here last night since you've been here so long?" Both police officers stepped a little closer to Eddie waiting for an answer.

"I haven't been here in a couple of days so I couldn't tell you a thing. What's going on? What's all this tape here for?" Eddie asked.

The first police officer looked back at the crime scene. "Looks like we've got ourselves a shooting. An elderly man was shot through the head. You know anything about that?"

"What the f....?" Eddie thought. "Oh no officer. Like I said, I haven't even been home." Eddie tried to look behind the officer to see who was shot. "Who is he?"

His question was ignored. "Where have you been? Doesn't look like you've been on a business trip." Both police officers chuckled.

Eddie tried to think of a lie. How the hell could he tell them he'd been on a drug binge and laying up with hookers for the past three days. "I was with one of my lady friends. Got a lil' caught up. You know what I mean?" Eddie tried give the police officers a mischievous smile.

They eyed Eddied suspiciously who couldn't stop fidgeting. Finally, one spoke up. "Lady friend huh? Well, look, if you hear anything, here's my card. Call me and I won't mention it was you. Wouldn't want anything happening to an upstanding fellow like yourself, would we?" He handed Eddie his business card while his partner coughed to hide his laugh.

Eddie was tired of being humiliated. He was still a man, after all. He reached out and took the card. "Can I go now officer?"

"Yeah, you can go." Both men went back to the crime scene.

Eddie hurried to get to his house. He didn't want the police officers to think of any more questions. "They said an old man died?"

Most of the people that circulated in this neck of the woods were young thugs conducting business on the corners or in the alleyways and young women willing to sell any part of their body for a fix.

"Old man? Old man?" Eddie racked his cloudy brain and it suddenly dawned on him. "Damn! I wonder if it was old man Ben. Matter of fact, I haven't see that nigga out there. He would have been the first one trying to see what happened."

Eddie fumbled with his key but couldn't get it in the lock because he was shaking so badly. He finally succeeded and hurried inside and slammed the door shut. He stood pressed up against the door until he could control his breathing.

"Who in the hell would kill Ben?" Eddie said aloud. "Sure, he was a rotten son-of-a-bitch but kill him?" Eddie shook his head trying to clear it.

He shuffled around trying to figure out where his life was headed. His son was showing signs of disrespect and his baby girl was being taken away from him. Damn if he didn't know that they had a long way to go but how could he fix it if she was gone? The only thing that made him happy that Ayanna was leaving was the fact that he was a junkie. He knew it; had known it for a long time.

When Lynette had told him that she was taking Ayanna away, he had felt both pain and relief. He hadn't quite been able to hide the brief moment of relief from showing in his face. He was almost positive that Lynette had seen it.

Eddie continued to shuffle around doing nothing in particular when he finally noticed that his stomach was growling. He hadn't eaten in days and he suddenly felt like he was going to pass out if he didn't put something on his stomach. He ate a bologna and cheese sandwich, not bothering to fry the bologna, and took off his shoes so he could lie down. Before lying down, however, something caught the corner of his eye. On top of his magazines was a baggie with a tiny white cube inside.

"Where did you come from?" Eddie's mouth salivated as he picked it up, but then tried to shake it off. "No! No! I can't fuck with you!" He yelled and held the baggie away from him.

He got up to flush it in the toilet but changed his mind and dropped the baggie in the trash. He paused as he was walking away. "Maybe I'll just save it just in case I might need a little something." Eddie thought.

He fished the baggie out of the trash can and put it in his cabinet. When he went back to the couch he was sleep before his head fully hit the pillow.

Eddie awoke to loud banging on the door. It took him a moment to register where he was and he couldn't figure out if the banging was at the door or in his head.

"Eddie, open the door! Are you in there?" A voice yelled from beyond the door.

Eddie was trying to move as slowly as possible but the banging persisted and he just wanted it to stop. "Hold up! Hold up! Stop that damn knocking!' He yelled as he shuffled to the door. Who is this at my....?"

As he opened the door, Diane cut him off. "Move out of my damn way, Eddie!" Diane said as she stormed inside. She looked around then put her hand over her nose. "This place is horrible and it stinks like hell."

Eddie shut the door. "Hello to you too sis." He pointed to the couch. "Why don't you sit your ass down? You're making me mad already."

Diane put her hand on her hip. "Nigga, you are triflin' as hell. Look how you're living? Did you know your daughter is in the State's custody?" Eddie looked at her wide-eyed. "Yeah that's right. Luckily, it's only temporary but you would've known that if your ass could stay out the crack houses long enough!"

She stared him down and he sat down on the couch slowly. Eddie stayed silent for a long time before he spoke. "What happened?" He asked slowly.

"Oh, now you care?" Diane huffed.

Eddie lost his temper. "Spare me your bullshit, Diane, and tell me what the fuck happened?"

His sister rolled her eyes. "Apparently Lynette's sister and daddy told some lies about her being unfit. We all know it ain't true, but Lynette said she's got to wait it out until she proves that she's fit to raise Ayanna." Diane looked around the room. "You should've been there to support Lynette."

As she walked to the door, she stopped to look back. "You know, you'd better be glad you're my brother or I would have cut you off a long time ago. Get your shit together or you're going to end up killing yourself."

With that last statement, Diane left leaving her brother staring sadly into empty space.

*****

Broken furniture littered the floor. Lynette had done her job thoroughly.

After Rita confessed to who was behind Ayanna being

taken away, Lynette had demanded that she take her straight to her sister's house.

"How dare this bitch come between me and my daughter?" Lynette thought angrily. "And daddy's not off the hook either. After all I've done for him?"

Rita kept looking back and forth between the road and her best friend. She could see the inner turmoil. "You've got to calm down Netty." Lynette gave her a deadly look and then stared straight ahead again. Rita chose not to say anything else.

Lynette shifted in her seat and looked out of the side window. When she spoke again, her voice cracked. "So much for family huh? Except for my daughter, that shit is overrated."

Rita gripped the steering wheel tighter. She wanted to go upside Lynda's head too; even had a few choice words for Andrew but she couldn't. She was the peacemaker.

They traveled the rest of the way in silence. When they finally reached Lynda's house. Rita was dismayed to find the driveway full of cars. "Damn. It looks like we crashed the party sis." She didn't budge from the car.

Lynette, on the other hand, didn't care who was there. The more the merrier in her eyes. That way everyone could witness the treachery that had caused her to go off the deep end. "Come on Rita. I don't have time to sit around waiting on you and your backbone." She got out of the car and slammed the door shut.

Rita got out of the car as quickly as she could manage. "That's not fair Lynette. Remember, I'm on your side."

Lynette just started walking up the door. She counted six cars in the driveway and all of them looked familiar. It looked like most of the gang was here but Lynette really didn't care. They had forgotten long ago that she was their sibling and not their child. Tonight, she would make them remember. She stormed up to the house, with Rita reluctantly in tow, and held down the doorbell. She could hear their voices inside which only fueled her anger.

Finally, the door opened. "Lynette, what are you doing here?" Simone stood there with her mouth open.

Lynette smirked. "Should've known that they could get in your head too." Lynette brushed past her. "You're so damn weak."

Simone almost closed the door on Rita before she realized that she was trying to come through. "You're here too?" She turned her attention back to her sister after Rita remained silent. "Who do you think you're talking to?"

Lynette threw up her hand. "I don't have time for you right now. I'm looking for the ringleader." She started walking in the direction of the den but Simone stepped in front of her.

"Don't go back there Netty. You're only asking for more trouble." Simone pleaded.

"Get out of my way Simone." When she didn't move, Lynette side-stepped her and started walking towards the den again with Simone and Rita arguing behind her.

"What the hell did you bring her here for? What kind of mess are you trying to pull?"

"I didn't do anything! We didn't even know everybody was here. She just wanted to see Lynda. What was I supposed to do?'

"Not bring her here?"

Lynette blocked them out as she made her way to the den. She didn't even break her stride as she pushed open the door."

"Well lookie here, it's a family affair. What? I wasn't invited?"

Five pairs of bewildered eyes looked up at Lynette at once. Her heart sank when she saw her brother Bobby also sitting with the rest of the group. He was always her favorite. He must have sensed how hurt she was since he kept avoiding her eyes.

Lynda was the first to recover from her shock. "I want you out of my house! You have no reason to be here but to start trouble!" She screamed as she stood up.

Lynette stayed rooted where she was. "I'm not going no damn where!" She looked around the room at her siblings; none of which had yet to say a word to her. "It looks like trouble has already started." Lynette walked up to Lynda and got nose to nose with her sister. "Starting with my daughter being taken away from me." She shoved Lynda back on the couch.

"Woooah! Woooah!" Bobby jumped up and grabbed Lynette. "You need to calm down lil' sis."

She quickly shook him off. "Don't touch me. What do you know about how Lynda and daddy lied on me and got Ayanna taken from me? Huh?" She narrowed her eyes. "Were you in on it too? Did you take part in the lies too big brother?" Lynette started pummeling her brother upside the head and chest.

Bobby grabbed both his sister's wrists and bear hugged her so she couldn't move. "Calm the fuck down! I just found out what was going on when Lynda called me."

Lynette looked over at her sister who was glued to the couch. It was funny to her how tough Lynda always acted and when it came down to it she had no fight in her. "Let me go. I'm not going to do anything."

"I swear you better not try any shit when I let you go." Bobby warned.

"Alright now. I wouldn't do it if I were you, Bobby. She might go upside your head again." Anthony chuckled.

"Shut up, Ant. Nobody's talking to you, anyway. I'm mad at you too!"

Anthony just shook his head. "You don't want none sis." He looked over at Lynda. "You alright over there? What the hell you call us over her for anyway? This is entertaining and all but I've got better things to do."

She tried her best to gain her composure and stood up again. "First of all, don't ever put your hands on me again. Second, I warned you that I wouldn't let you corrupt Ayanna. You run the streets, you're never home, and you're always pawning her off on somebody else. You taking my baby to North Carolina is the last straw. I will do whatever it takes to make sure that Ayanna is well taken care of." Lynda looked around the room. "That's why I called everybody over here because I need it to be a family effort in order for Ayanna to be given to me. We know her daddy ain't worth two cents so he won't be able to get her."

Simone came running in the room with Rita in tow. "I'm sorry, Lynda. I couldn't stop her."

Lynda waved her off. "I should have known better." She stared down Rita. "I see Lynette's side-kick is here. What are you supposed to prove by being here?"

Rita shook her finger at Lynda. "Uh uh. Don't' start no mess with me. I'm here to support your sister which apparently you don't know how to do. I'm staying right here. Now try and move me." She crossed her arms and didn't budge.

Catheryn finally spoke up much to the dismay of their

brother Donnell. He usually avoided confrontation at all costs and had spent the entire time trying to figure out how to make a hasty exit.

"This is ridiculous. Lynette, we are doing what we think is best for Ayanna…"

"Don't put me in this shit. This is the first time I've heard of this mess." Anthony cut her off.

Catheryn smacked her lips. "Well that was what we were supposed to be discussing tonight before Lynette busted up in here like she owned the place."

"How the hell is being in the State's care the 'best for Ayanna' is what I want to know!" Lynette screamed. "Because of your lies, my baby is in a place where none of us can protect her. Can't you see what the hell you've done?" She got in Lynda's face. "I want you to go down to the State's office and let them know that what you said wasn't true. I want my damn daughter back!"

Lynda flinched but stood her ground. "I'm not doing a damn thing! I've already got plans so that I can get Ayanna out and get temporary guardianship."

"Damn sis. You're really going all out. Netty might like to smoke a lil' bit but who doesn't? She a cool ass mom and my lil' niece always happy." Anthony shook his head at his sister.

"I'm with Ant." Bobby spoke up. "If I would've known I was coming here for this shit, I would have stayed with my lady."

Anthony laughed. "I know that's right. I've got a lil' tender waiting on me too. What about you Donnie?"

Donnell just waved him off.

Lynda was furious. "I don't give a damn. Simone and Catheryn will help me. I'm sorry I even called you over here."

"You know what….." Lynette ran out of the room. Shortly afterwards there was the sound of crashing and cracking. Everyone ran in the living room to see lamps being broken against the wall and Lynette stomping on the upside-down table leg breaking it off.

"What the hell are you doing? Are you crazy?" Lynda lunged at Lynette trying to stop her from fully breaking the leg.

But Lynette just flung her sister off of her in a rage. "You want to take away my baby then I'm going to take away all the shit you love too!" She yelled as the leg finally separated from the table.

"Come on Netty! You need to stop this. Breaking up everything is not going to bring Ayanna home." Rita's statement went unnoticed.

Lynette continued her rampage while her sister attempted to get up from the floor. "This looks like it's worth something so it's got to go too!" She shattered a heavy wall mirror with the table leg.

"Now you know you need to cut this shit out." Donnell warned and took a step towards Lynette.

"Don't even think about coming near me." She grabbed a large piece of glass with her free hand.

Donnell jumped back. "Woah! Have you lost your mind? I know you not about to cut me."

"Don't try me Donnie." Lynette glared at her brother. "Y'all are always trying to run me. Tell Lynda to get my daughter back or I'm breaking all this shit up.

Lynda didn't move so Lynette proceeded to break everything in the bookcase. "I'm calling the damn police if you don't get out of my house right now. And don't you bring your ass back here either."

"You best believe, if I don't get Ayanna back before the end of this week, I'm going to be back and it's not going to be a friendly visit. Lynette threw down the table leg. "Come on Rita, I'm ready to go." and she stomped out the front door with Rita behind her.

Lynda looked around and started crying while her sisters and brothers helped collect broken pieces of furniture. Everyone had forgotten about Andrew who had been in the back room witnessing the entire scene unfold with a shameful heart.

*****

"How did I not know my baby girl wasn't safe?" Eddie thought as he leaned back on the couch. He had locked himself in his room for most of the day replaying the news his sister had delivered to him in his mind.

"You should've been there to support Lynette." He could still hear her words loud and clear.

"Get your shit together or you're going to end up killing yourself." Eddie had given himself the same advice too many times but still couldn't shake the urge; could never quite get control of the beast. Even now, the hunger was growing.

Eddie shook his head trying to clear it. He just needed something to get him going again. Too many events had transpired, leaving his mind even more clouded than it had been before. Slowly, he walked the short distance to the kitchen to try and find food. Opening the refrigerator, he grimaced when a pungent smell hit his nose and he quickly shut the door. He doubted he had anything in the cabinets but he decided to look anyway. Maybe there was a can of Spam he had forgotten somewhere. He was rummaging through the remaining cabinets when his fingers touched a plastic bag. Eddie couldn't believe his eyes. He had completely forgotten about his hidden treasure.

"This is just what the doctor ordered." Eddie smiled as he looked at the white cube; the answer to his immediate needs. He did a dance as he proceeded to go about his business preparing to get high. Finally, he had tied himself off and his spoon was suspended in air with its contents getting liquefied. Suddenly, gunfire shot off in the distance scaring Eddie. As a result, he dropped the spoon and its contents on the nasty table in front of him. He watched, horrified, as clear liquid ran all over the table's sticky contents.

"No! No! No! This shit ain't happening!"

Eddie knew there was no way to salvage what would have taken him far away; at least for a short time. He looked over at the plastic bag and saw there was a small piece of the crack left. He hurried and liquefied it with his lighter and shot what little of what was left into his veins. He sighed and leaned back on his couch while the drug took effect. After a few minutes, he started thinking about what was going on in his life. He was a drug addict, Ayanna had been taken away and he could do nothing, he was now out of a job, his family had disowned him. The list went on and on. At the top of that list, however, was Sweetman. The man who constantly threatened him and was the cause, in his mind, of all his problems. If Sweetman wasn't riding him all of the time, then Eddie wouldn't have fell off the wagon. Well, he would make him pay for messing up his life. He was invincible. Eddie looked around the room with wild eyes. The more he thought about his life, the angrier he became. He could see everything clearer now and felt like he could take over the world.

"I'm going to make you pay for fuckin' up my life you rich pig!" Eddie yelled.

He knocked over the table and stood up with his fists clenched. "Yeah. I'm going to make you pay and get my life back." Eddie said eerily, barely speaking aloud. He clinched and unclenched his fist one more time before he grabbed his keys and ran out the door.

Sixteenth Chapter

A week had passed and Ayanna was officially over what she considered a jail sentence. She had resisted all attempts at the councilors trying to make her "open up". Ayanna had gone to one councilor when she had first arrived and nothing had come of it, obviously, because she still hadn't been able to go home or even talk to her mother. What could possibly be the reason that they would keep her away from her mother? She had scraped at the windowsill for hours but no matter how hard she had tried, the window would not open. No amount of pounding on the window and crying would work. Ayanna had decided to wait until she was escorted to one of her sessions and she would tell what really happened.

"How are you doing today, Ayanna?" The older lady across the desk asked.

Ayanna had never met her before and glanced at the plaque on the wall. It read Rebecca Stokely Ph.D. Ayanna wasn't impressed. How did this lady think she was doing? She was in a prison. "I'm fine." She mumbled and picked a spot on the desk to stare at.

The doctor leaned forward and smiled. "I can't begin to imagine how difficult this is so I know you're not fine. I'm

Dr. Stokely. I know that we don't know each other, but please know that you can talk to me."

Ayanna continued to stare at nothing in particular on the desk and kept her mouth closed. How could she know if this lady would really listen to her and do something so she could go home?

Rebecca tried a different tactic. "I bet you're ready to go back to your school. I know hanging around with a bunch of know-it-all adults gets pretty boring. Trust me I know." She said and smiled politely.

Ayanna wasn't buying into the doctor fully but she was starting to warm up to her just a little. She seemed to be somewhat genuine but Ayanna knew better. "If I say yes, can I go home?" She asked smugly.

Dr. Stokely's smile wavered for a moment. "I'm afraid that is out of my control."

"Then why am I here?" Ayanna asked through clenched teeth. "If you can't help me then I might as well go back to my room."

"I'm here because I'm concerned about your welfare. If your mother is doing anything to harm you then my job is to protect you from it"

"My mom isn't doing anything!" Ayanna yelled. "Why does everybody keep blaming my mom for me being here? It's my uncle who's the mean one!"

Dr. Stokely leaned forward calmly. She was used to outbursts in her line of work. "What does your uncle have to do with this? You can talk to me."

"Are you going to do something about it?"

"If there is something going on that would put you in danger then, yes, I will make sure that something gets done."

Dr. Stokely replied calmly. "What's on your mind? I'm listening."

Ayanna hoped that she really would.

She hadn't heard anything since that visit, so she figured that everyone was still just pretending to care. She had been curled up on her cot for the past few days. She refused to come out to the common room and eat, so her trays of food had started showing up outside of her door. She had no clue who it was and didn't care but it did ensure that she ate three meals a day. She missed her brother. She missed her cousins. She missed her grandfather. But most of all, she missed her mother. No one understood or believed in their bond. Most of the other mothers of her school friends were stay at home moms who fussed over their kids and never had any real fun. Of course, her friends went to the movies, out to eat, or to relative's houses on Sundays. But Ayanna and her mother went to the best house parties in the city. There would always be a few more kids her age whose parents were at the party too. Of course, Ayanna wasn't allowed to participate in all of the "grownup" activities but everyone knew that she could dance and when the music got turned up, she was always invited to join. She could still smell the incense and fried chicken, hear the horns from Earth Wind and Fire, and see the smiles from her mother's friends as she danced in the circle they'd formed. She even missed the drive back home from the city as they laughed about what had happened at the party that night. They also went to free plays in the park and live ballets. They would spread out a blanket on the stone steps and nibble on chicken salad sandwiches while the dancers held her gaze. These were private moments just for them because no one else enjoyed their activities the way the two of them did. They would even curl up on the couch with freshly baked cookies and watch black and white movies. Her mother never missed a beat when Ayanna asked her about her childhood. She had learned from all of Lynette's stories that her mother was no angel and was just as rebellious as she was. No wonder her grandfather always said that they were just alike. Lynette understood what she felt like living with her grandfather and uncle. She would tell Ayanna to stay strong because she was Lynette's backbone. She would tell Ayanna that she had courage and mattered in this world no matter the circumstances she was born into. She was a young mother so Lynette still remembered what it was like as a preteen and that meant the world to Ayanna. What her family saw as a too young, irresponsible mother; Ayanna saw as a relatable carefree mother and she wouldn't have it any other way. Everyone would just have to get over it.

She was staring up at the ceiling, counting the water spots when someone knocked on her door. She didn't bother to answer but the door opened anyway.

"Is there any privacy around here?" Ayanna asked without bothering to see who it was in her room.

"Most of the children here sleep two to three to a room. I say you're getting plenty of privacy young lady."

Ayanna head snapped around to see who the person was and saw that it was Olivia Reynolds. She hadn't seen the social worker since the day she was brought here. "How did I get so lucky?"

Olivia sighed. "Ayanna, I'm not the enemy. My job is to protect you not make you like me. I did, however, request that you be put in a room alone. Most of the other children here come from really horrific homes and as a result it can get rough sometimes. I didn't think that you would be safe in that environment."

Ayanna looked away. "Thank you."

Olivia took a step forward. "I'm here with good news, Ayanna. You're going home today."

Ayanna couldn't believe her ears. "Are you serious? I'm really going home?"

"Yes. Your mom and, I believe, your aunt are here to pick you up. Go ahead and get your belongings together so we can go out to the lobby and meet them."

Ayanna jumped off her cot and gathered the few belongings she had taken quickly from home. She ran out the door, with Olivia yelling behind her to slow down, and skidded into the lobby where her Lynette and her aunt Diane were waiting.

"Ma!" She yelled as she flew into her mother's arms.

"You don't know how much I missed you baby." Lynette said through tears as she squeezed Ayanna in a tight hug.

Olivia appeared in the room. She stood back discreetly as the trio embraced each other. Finally, Lynette wiped her eyes and saw the social worker standing awkwardly to the side.

"Ms. Reynolds, is it?" Serves her right if she's uncomfortable. Lynette thought.

Olivia sighed. "Yes, Ms. Lee." She looked over at Ayanna. "I came here to make sure that your daughter was signed out properly and to also ensure that she was released only in your care. You're free to go and take Ayanna home where she belongs. I will have to conduct a few follow-up visits but I don't anticipate any problems when it comes to your parenting skills. You seem like you are a great mother."

There was silence for a few moments before Diane spoke up. "Damn Netty, at least tell the woman thank you for getting my niece out of this hell hole."

"She's the one who put her in here!" Lynette pointed out.

"Ma can we go please?" Ayanna pleaded with her mother.

Lynette rolled her eyes at Olivia before turning to her daughter. "Of course, baby. Let's go home."

*****

Andrew was sneaking out of the outhouse where he kept one of his secret stashes when he heard the crunching of the gravel driveway. He had avoided Lynette since that fateful day at Linda's house when Lynette had damn near lost her mind. He was still disturbed by that scene. It's what caused him to go to Social Services to give the truth on what had actually been going on. It pained him to confess that his daughter didn't tell the whole truth. He was able to get them not to press charges on her by convincing the authorities that she was misled by Jerome and was only looking out for Ayanna.

High-pitched laughter made its way to Andrew's ears. "Ma, I can't believe I'm home! I didn't think I was ever getting out."

Andrew looked down and smiled. His baby girl was home and he couldn't be happier. He had to mend his relationship with his daughter after he gave Lynette and Ayanna some time together. There was no way he could go on like this. Rita had come over shaking her finger at him telling him how ashamed of himself he should be. God, how he loved that woman. She had practically grown up under his roof. But damn if she wasn't bossy as hell; had been that way since she was a little girl.

"You ought to be ashamed of yourself! How in the world could you let Lynda convince you to go against Lynette like that? Do you realize the harm you've done?" Rita had yelled.

Andrew had been trying to hide behind the tool shed when he had spotted her marching down the road. It was too late. She had already spotted him. "I'm not trying to hear no mess from you today. I got enough on my mind."

Rita had no intention of backing down. "You can't get rid of me that easy. Sister against sister, father against daughter, niece against aunt; the family is being torn apart!"

"Didn't I tell you to leave me the hell alone?" Andrew roared making Rita step back. She was used to him being an angry drunk but him getting angry while sober was a different story. Andrew paced back and forth shaking his head. "I just didn't want my baby to be taken away from me. I didn't mean for all of this to happen. Damn. I thought they would give Ayanna to Lynda for a minute but turns out I was wrong. I don't know nothing about the system." He took a deep breath. "I'll make this right. I got to."

Rita still didn't feel any sympathy for Andrew. Ayanna was her goddaughter and she was angry. "Well I hope you do something real soon because Netty wants her child back and she's going to do whatever it takes to get her back whether you like the way she does it or not."

So, Andrew had done something about it and now his granddaughter was home. He couldn't face her. Not yet. He had expected Lynette to let him have it, but not a word had been said to him. He didn't blame her and it was better that way. He figured she just didn't have the energy to call him out on his actions. He wasn't about to open up that dialog any time soon. For now, he was content to see Ayanna happy again. If he knew his granddaughter well, when she was ready, she would definitely seek him out. Andrew was still trying to figure out how to handle that encounter when it finally did happen. When the duo giggled their way into the house, Andrew came out from his hiding spot and smiled. "Welcome home baby. Welcome home."

*****

Eddie paced the street not far from where Sweetman lived. He had been on a serious high and wanted more: but not before he took out his anger and frustration on Sweetman and his minion. Eddie didn't know which one he hated most. Big Mike would test his resolve every time he was around while the fat boss just sat back and sneered. Eddie had had enough. He wanted his life back and this was the only way that he knew how. He had already visited one of his old friends from when he was on top of his game. His friend, Tyrone, had been a jokester but could also be a hothead if provoked. He had always been loyal and was one of the few from the old gang that hadn't succumbed to the streets either by drugs, jail, or sometimes merciful death. Tyrone specialized in obtaining illegal guns that couldn't be traced. It had been almost a decade since they had seen each other but when they saw each other, it was as if no time had passed.

"Hey man! Long time no see. Where the hell you been?" Tyrone was grinning from ear to ear as he opened the screen door for his old friend. HIs smile faltered, however, when he took a closer look.

Eddie could barely look him in the eye because he knew

he looked bad but he forced himself to stand up straight. Tyrone despised weakness which was one of the reasons he had respected Eddie. Eddie wasn't trying to change that in any way. "It's been a minute man. I was in the neighborhood and I said, 'let me go see my old partner in crime.'" He stretched out his hand.

"Yeah man. A'ight. Whatever you say." Tyrone stretched out his hand to give his old friend a pound. "Come on in man."

Tyrone led Eddie to one of the plush couches in his spacious living room. Eddie looked around the room and took in all of the expensive décor. "Damn, man it looks like you've done pretty well for yourself."

Tyrone lit up a Newport, leaned back on the couch, and smiled. "Yeah, you can say that. I saved up a little money from the old days, started dabbling in a little bit of this and a little bit of that, and managed to accumulate what you see before you." Tyrone spread out his arms and laughed.

Eddie chuckled but didn't say anything in response.

"So let's cut out all the bullshit. I know you just didn't happen to be in the neighborhood like you said, man." Tyrone took a pull of his cigarette. "Looks like you're bobbing and weaving a lil' bit. What? You took up a new hobby since I last saw you?"

Eddie couldn't keep still. He just wanted to get what he came for and be on his way. He didn't have time to explain himself or go back down memory lane.

Tyrone shook his head slowly and continued. "I haven't seen you in damn near ten years and now you wanna suddenly pop up to just shoot the breeze for old time's sake? Man, come on. You know I like to clown around but I ain't nobody's fool."

Tyrone set his glass down on the table and leaned back on the couch waiting for Eddie's reply.

Eddie chuckled before dropping his head in defeat. "You're right, man. I done hit rock bottom. But that's not why I'm here. I gotta plan that's gonna make it alright again!" Eddie looked up and narrowed his eyes at his old friend. "But I need the kind of help that only you can give me."

There was silence between the two for a few minutes before Tyrone spoke first. "I'm gonna need the rest of the story before I get involved in anything. I've been running my 'business' pretty tight without any bullshit coming back to me so far."

Eddie shook his head and started wringing out his hands in frustration. "I get it man. I just don't have time to be sitting around telling stories like we in kindergarten."

Tyrone leaned forward. "Well nigga I guess you better dim the lights and get ready for story time if you want my help." He picked up his glass and swallowed the last of his drink. "So, what's it gonna be?"

Eddie was growing more restless by the minute. He threw up his hands. "Alright man. Damn. See, I've been dealing with this cat from the West End…"The story was summarized with Eddie perpetrated as the innocent victim. He was simply a man trying to look out for his family.

Tyrone had lived his life on the streets so he knew how to fill in the missing pieces and weed out the parts that weren't true. Eddie knew this about him but he had tested him anyway. "You know what man? You done come a long way from when we used to run things back in the day. You had your head on straight. You had the nice clothes, cars, and plenty of girls. You were smart about your money, man. You know what else? You were smart about what you put in your body. You might smoke a lil' green every now and then but that's it. You think I don't see a junkie sitting in front of me?"

"Wait a damn minute!" Eddie interrupted.

"Man, fuck that! You high right now! Just admit that shit. I'm your friend."

Eddie jumped up. "Look. I'm not trying to get into all that. I came here because I need some juice. Something light and easy to hide. I'll make sure that nothing comes back on you, man. I swear." Eddie cleared his throat when Tyrone didn't respond. "I don't have no cash either, man. I was hoping you could do this for me for old time's sake."

Tyrone threw his head back and laughed. "For old time's sake? Here we go again. I've already done time for you. If anyone should be asking for favors, it should be me."

Eddie took a step forward. "I know you're not trying to bring that old shit up. You did what a second in command was supposed to do and you took the heat a couple of times. I had to keep things running smooth. I couldn't trust anybody to else to take over while I was sitting in jail. Get out of here with that shit."

"Don't try to run up on me in my own house!" Tyrone jumped up from the couch. "You're right. I'm not a fuckin snitch and I never will be but you could've shown me more love while I was doing time for you and you didn't show my family no love while I was in the joint either. Do you remember that? Now you want to run up in my house demanding favors? Man, get the hell out of here. You're blowing my mellow mood."

Eddie sighed and started backing up towards the door. "Look. I didn't mean no harm, man, by coming here. I just figured you could throw me a bone and help me out. But, I'm leaving."

Before Eddie could touch the door knob, Tyrone stopped him. "Man, we go back a long time and we used to be tight so I'm going to help you out this one time. I don't like whatever this is that you became, man. After this, I don't want to see your ass no more. You got that?"

"Yeah man I got it."

"Good. Then let me get another drink and then I'll introduce you to my friends."

*****

"Is this what you had in mind bro?"

Tyrone had taken Eddie down into his basement where all of his artillery was stored. Eddie started wringing his hands again when his friend removed the floorboards revealing a host of weapons to choose from.

"Damn! You've come up over the years. Your paper must be real long doing this shit."

Tyrone smirked. "I do alright man."

Eddie shook his head. "Damn that. You doin' more than just alright"

"Well don't worry about my business. You see something you like? The serial numbers are already taken care of."

Still feeling good from the coke he had earlier, Eddie felt a burst of exhilaration as he looked down at his choices. He could get in and get out and no one would ever suspect it was him. Not Eddie the junkie. Hopefully, everyone would automatically assume it was a rival or personal enemy of Sweetman's. He had made his fair share of decisions over the years that had left more than one child fatherless or mother childless. How many other lives had been destroyed? Eddie wondered. He felt there was no way anyone could trace Sweetman's death back to him

"You alright, man? You need me to pick one for you?"

Tyrone's voice broke up Eddie's thoughts. "Yeah. I'm good. I was just trying to think so I can make sure I do this shit right." He looked down at his choices again. He licked his lips and smiled. "Let me get that one. It's perfect."

*****

Sweetman was sitting alone in his office when he heard a knock at the door. It could have been only one person. "Come on in Big Mike." He watched as the massive frame stepped into the room casting a temporary shadow. "You ever considered going on a diet?"

"Never crossed my mind." Was the quick reply followed by a rare smile.

Sweetman leaned back in his chair. "So what are you doing in my office? Everything alright?"

Big Mike puffed out his chest. "One of my boys spotted Eddie coming out of Tyrone's place earlier."

Sweetman shifted in his chair. "What! I thought I had taken care of that nigga! That old man assured me that he had put the goods right where Eddie could see it. Hell, as much as he shoots and snorts, we should have already seen in the obituaries." Sweetman shook his head. "You said he was seen coming out of Tyrone's?"

Big Mike nodded. "That's what my boy said. He was on his way to make a drop when he saw Eddie. Eddie didn't see him though. It didn't seem too strange since they used to run together but I figured you should know anyway."

"Damn! You just don't get it?" Sweetman leaned forward.

"Tyrone is one of the biggest 'gun collectors' in the South East. I know they haven't talked for a long time so something must be up or going down. Either way, I've got to be prepared. I forgot that junkie used to have friends."

Big Mike was ready for some excitement. "What do you want me to do boss?"

"I don't know if and when that fool is going to try to come at me so, just in case, I want you to be by my side at all times and armed. I've got too much to lose and I'll be damned if I let that nigga take it away from me."

"Oh, you don't have to worry about that." The big man patted the small of his back and then lifted up his pant leg. "I'm always prepared. I'm going to put a few extra guys on house detail. They can let me know if they see any signs of Eddie."

"Good thinking. Good thinking. Now all we need to do is wait and see what move he makes on me. I'll be ready though. Believe that."

After Sweetman had been left alone, He lit his signature cigar, leaned back and started thinking about the situation unfolding around him.

"Son of a bitch! So, you want to play in the major leagues, huh?"

He had tried to get rid of Eddie quietly. No mess. No fuss. Just a man dying from what everybody expected him to die from. Sweetman had grown tired of the games and couldn't even remember why he had cared so much about what he had witnessed all those years ago. The young sexy woman he had obsessed over in his mind for so many years didn't even know he existed; would never feel for him what he felt for her. Now it was just about getting rid of the filth that surrounded him.

To him, people like Eddie were the dregs of the Earth. All they did was take from people and inflict pain on everyone around them like an incurable disease. Leeches were what they were and needed to be gotten rid of. Eddie would be made an example of. Sweetman had been made fun of for the better part of his younger life by people like Eddie. Those who had everything to live for and appreciated none of it. Sweetman despised him. He still remembered Ayanna's face when he had seen her and her crafty little friend at the mall. He smiled at the thought of her friend. If taught properly, she could do well working for him. But Ayanna was a different story. She was smart but she wasn't street savvy. She was still innocent and Sweetman knew that Eddie didn't give a damn and he if he did, he had no clue how to show it. The only thing worth anything was his next fix. He had been tested and, as expected, had failed. Sweetman knew what he was doing when he had brought Eddie back into his fold. The intention was not to see if he failed but rather when he would fail. For a moment, Sweetman had thought that Eddie would actually pull through but a push here and there set him back on his downward slide again.

"Alright nigga. Let' get this over with."

*****

Eddie felt as if his heart was about to beat out of his chest. He had tucked the gun in the small of his back and was preparing himself to give the secret knock that would allow him to enter his nemesis' home. Eddie had never given away his true feelings toward Sweetman and was hoping that he wouldn't have any trouble gaining entry to carry out his plans. His only mission was to get close enough to finish him and Big Mike, who was certain to be not too far away from his boss, off. Wiping that smug smile off Mike's face made Eddie's heart skip a beat. How many times had he been humiliated by the big man? Eddie always found himself having to sidestep the snide comments that were always on the tip of Mike's tongue. There would be no more humiliation after today and he would start a new life somewhere else. He would make sure he gained back the respect of his family and friends; but most of all, his children.

Eddie's high was coming down but that didn't stop his determination for what he was about to do. He raised his hand slowly and knocked. Knocked. He knocked again. And then he knocked the final time. After a brief moment, he heard the familiar silent click signaling him to enter. Eddie took a deep breath and then opened the door.

"I hope there's a good reason why you decided to show up unannounced."

Eddie instinctively looked in the direction of Sweetman's desk but saw no one there. The room was dimly lit so it took him a moment for his eyes to adjust. He finally saw Sweetman sitting on the end of his plush couch; one hand on his lap and the other lazily draped over the back of the couch. For once, there was no cigar burning which was odd to Eddie.

"Well? I like to get all of the facts before I hand down my sentence." Sweetman shifted slightly.

"I got some things I need to get off my chest and I wanted to do it personally." Eddie looked around. "Where's your body guard? I'm surprised he isn't up your ass right now."

Sweetman smirked. "A little bold today, huh? He's around. So, what do you have to get off your chest that was so important that you had to interrupt my day?"

Eddie didn't trust Sweetman but he had gotten himself this far so he wasn't about to back down now. "I've put in work for you for a minute but now I'm here to tell you that I'm done. No more lookouts, no more counting money, no more having to come to you for nothing. I can't do this anymore, man."

"I didn't tell you that you could get out, did I? I least I don't remember that conversation." Sweetman's voice was like ice as he leaned forward.

Eddie backed up instinctively but pressed on as he got angrier. "Look, I'm not asking for your permission. I'm a grown ass man. You know what? I'm sick of your shit anyway. You sit behind your big ass desk in your ivory tower judging every damn body. I bust my ass making sure your money doesn't come up short and you treat me like shit every time I come around you." Eddie got hysterical. "You were supposed to help me, black man, but you didn't do anything but make me sicker. My kids don't even respect me and you know what? It's all your fault. Nigga fuck you!" Eddie pulled the gun from the small of his back and quickly took aim at Sweetman. A gunshot went off, and then everything went silent.

"What the fuck?" Eddie's eyes were wide as he looked down and saw blood coming from his right side. He staggered as he tried to find something to lean on but finding nothing, sat down hard on the floor.

"You alright, boss?" A small voice came from the shadows.

Sweetman looked at Eddie and then in the direction of the voice. "Yes. You did good."

"Thank you, boss."

He stood up and walked over to where Eddie was sitting on the floor. "So you thought that you could come into my home and take me out? Really? Man, your mind is worse than

I thought." Sweetman leaned down close to Eddie's face. "You need to leave that shit alone." He laughed and then called for his bodyguard. "Big Mike, get in here so we can take care of this situation. I've got better things to do with my day."

Eddie was sitting on the floor panting heavily when Big Mike entered the room. "Looks like the new recruit did a pretty good job."

"Yeah but now it's time to finish this."

"What do you want done?" Big Mike asked as he looked down on a shaking Eddie.

"Just do what you do best and get rid of him. The river should do nicely."

Eddie started pleading. "Come on man, let me go. I'm already fucked up." He grabbed Sweetman's leg. "I wasn't going to shoot you man. I just wanted out that's all."

Sweetman shook him off. "Get off me! You wanted out so now you're going to get your wish. You ain't shit and your kids will be better off without your junkie ass!" He turned to Big Mike. "Get rid of him and do it quick. Make sure everything is cleaned up thoroughly. I don't want him tied back to me at all. Understood?"

"Understood."

Sweetman glanced at Eddie one more time before he walked out the room with Eddie's pleas still calling behind him.

Big Mike called over the recruit. "One in the head. No exceptions, to make sure he's dead. Can you handle that?

"Yes."

Big Mike smiled. "Then carry on."

Kenya couldn't have been prouder of herself as she aimed and squeezed the trigger ending her first life.

Seventeenth Chapter

"Man, sis. What was it like up in the joint? Did you have to do something perverted just to stay alive? Come on. You can tell me. I promise I won't tell anybody without getting a hefty fee upfront."

Ayanna and Cedric were sitting on the porch at their Aunt Diane's house watching the neighborhood kids play in the front yard across the street.

Ayanna punched her brother in the arm. "Shut up stupid! It wasn't even like that." Cedric dodged as Ayanna threw another punch.

"I'd be worried if I were you with that left hook." Cedric laughed as Ayanna continued to scowl but then grew serious. "For real though sis. I missed you and I got to admit I was a little worried what might happen to you around a bunch of crazy delinquents."

Ayanna shrugged. "It wasn't as bad as you might think. They kept me separated from the rest of the girls. The worst part was not being able to go home every day or even know when you might get to go home. I hated not knowing. Then the councilors acting all fake like they really care about you. I couldn't wait to get out of that place."

"Why were you even there in the first place? One day you

were just gone and nobody would talk around me." Cedric shook his head puzzled.

"I think it had something to do with my uncle. You know how bad things are at my house. That's why we have to move in the first place. I told the councilors what was going on and my mom was innocent. I guess they must have found out I was telling the truth and let me go home." Ayanna stood up and started pacing. "I still don't understand though. I heard my mom on the phone saying she never wanted to see my aunt again but I don't know why. She barely looks at my granddaddy or even speak to him so I'm really confused. He looks sad all the time and my mom looks mad all the time. It's worse living there than it was before. I wanted to go home but not if it's going be like this. I'd rather just stay here at Aunt Diane's until we move to North Carolina."

"Sis, I get it but you've got to toughen up."

"What do you mean I've got to tough...."

"Hold on a minute." Cedric interrupted.

"What?" Ayanna snapped.

"Look. All I'm trying to say is I know it's bad at your house but you know that your granddaddy depends on you. Didn't you tell me once that you were the only one who really cared and wanted to protect him? He's already going to be without you when you move. I'm just saying that he might like it if you stuck around until you move. You know what I mean?"

Ayanna shrugged her shoulders and looked away. "You might have a point. I hide his liquor and make him sandwiches so I can make sure he eats..." Ayanna suddenly got a faraway look in her eyes. "And protect him from my uncle."

Cedric's face changed to concern. "You alright sis?"

"Yeah I'm alright. I was just thinking out loud..." Ayanna tried to perk herself up. "Look, I don't have that much longer in Richmond and I don't want to spend the rest of the time thinking about all the bad stuff. Let's just have some fun and I can practice my left hook on you."

Cedric laughed. "Yeah you better work on it because if you don't somebody's going to lay you out with all that lip you got."

"Whatever! I wish they would. Besides, I can pretty much talk my way out of anything anyway. My mom says it's a gift."

"Yeah okay. But hey listen." Cedric paused for a moment. "I've got to ask. Are you going to talk to Pops before you go off into the sunset?"

Ayanna shook her head. "I don't know. I guess I should. He was doing alright for a minute but I just don't know. I guess I should at least say bye, huh?"

"I mean...If you want to. I'm not going to tell you what to do but it wouldn't hurt. He might be kind of mad if you just left without at least saying something to him."

"Well he hasn't said anything to me for years before I met him so I don't owe him nothing. I'll think about it but I don't want to talk about it anymore."

Cedric threw up his hands. "Alright. Suit yourself. I'm just saying."

"Well how about you don't say anything else. I'm hungry anyway." She stood up and stretched. "I can smell fried chicken. That's probably why I'm hungry. What about you?"

"Oh yeah. Diane can fry some chicken."

"Alright well let's go get on her nerves then." Ayanna grabbed the screen door handle before looking back at her brother. "Remember. I don't want to talk about Eddie anymore. I'll figure something out."

"I got you, sis. I got you."

*****

"Where in the world could he possibly be? Probably in a damn gutter somewhere." Lynette thought.

She had been searching for Eddie for days. She had gone to his job but had quickly learned from his supervisor that Eddie had not been seen in a week and if she did see him to tell him not to bother coming back. Calls had gone unanswered and visits to his home had proved useless. None of his family members had seen him. Diane had admitted that she had gone to see him a few days before and went off on him but hadn't seen him or heard from him since. "When will you ever stop being a disappointment?" She had wanted to talk to Eddie one last time about Ayanna leaving. Everything in her bones told Lynette to just walk away but she would be damned if she would ever allow Eddie to be able to throw anything in her face later. She was going to simply let him know that as long as he stayed clean he would be able to see his daughter with no problems. Ayanna had never indicated to Lynette that Eddie was doing anything wrong and had even commented that he had a comical side. Lynette had secretly rolled her eyes. But she also knew that more than anything else, her daughter would mostly miss her newfound family. Her brother, in particular, had brought a lot of joy to Ayanna's life. Lynette was grateful for that.

But for now, where the hell was Eddie? She would never admit it loud, but she was actually getting a little worried. Lynette leaned back in the lounge chair under the Weeping

Willow and closed her eyes. It was the time of the evening when the sky glowed with orange from the setting sun. She let the cool breeze envelope her, and for a moment, all her worries and fears slipped away. She would miss this when she moved away. Her eyes took in acres of fields where cats and mice ran wild and thick woods where deer made their hidden homes. Neighbors were a holler away and streets stayed clean. Would the air smell this fresh where she was moving? Would she be able to hear the crickets and cicadas singing in the hot evenings? And the stars. Would she be able to see sky lights with all of the city lights overpowering the view? Lynette smiled as she remembered countless times searching for star constellations on those truly clear nights. She thought of Michael. How she had missed him all these years. Anger would boil up inside of her from time to time when she thought of the circumstances surrounding his and Precious's death. Ayanna had asked about her friend for a while but Lynette kept reminding her that God simply needed her for other duties. Lynette sighed. So many memories with people she had known her entire life and now would be leaving it all behind.

Lynette pondered that for a moment until she thought of Marcus. He had awakened her with his patience, candor, and love. She had never experienced a man like Marcus before and she was praying that it would last. Her daughter was the final decision maker when it came to her mother's relationships and Ayanna knew this. Thankfully, Ayanna really liked Marcus and surprisingly both of his daughters, so Lynette felt like she was on a winning streak. He had helped Lynette find an apartment in a nice neighborhood after educating her on areas with the best schools. He had arranged for a moving company to pack her and Ayanna's belongings but Lynette had declined by telling him they could save money by doing it themselves. Marcus even brought her a local newspaper and a map of the city so she could know her surroundings and know what was going on before she moved.

Lynette heard the familiar sound of gravel crunching and turned her head to see a white Cadillac rolling slowly up the driveway. It could be no one else but her Aunt Susan, her mother's little sister. Lynette sighed. It wasn't often that her aunt was seen where she called 'country bumpkin land'. Her usually two to three times a year visits often consisted of snobbishly turning her nose up at everyone around her and reminding them secretly that they were beneath her. Lynette braced herself for the inevitable. The car stopped rolling and a tall regal middle-aged woman stepped out of the car. She looked around and sniffed the air for a moment before wrinkling her nose and taking a handkerchief out of her small and expensive handbag. She looked around until her eyes met Lynette's.

"My goodness! All this dust in the air is horrible for my allergies."

Lynette tried to suppress a smile but failed. "Well you are surrounded by dirt, Aunt Susan."

Susan glared her at niece. "I don't need any sass from you young lady. I just don't know how you all stay out here in the country. There's chickens running around for God's sake!"

Lynette stood. "It's nice to see you Aunt Susan. What brought you down to the country today? Your favorite nephew isn't here right now."

Susan walked over to the other chair and studied it

before sitting down. Lynette slowly sat back down in the chair beside her.

"You don't want to go in the house?" Lynette asked.

"No. I won't be staying long and I didn't come here to see your brother. I came here to talk to you." Susan stated matter-of-factly, not bothering to deny that Jerome was her favorite.

"What did you want to talk to me about?"

Susan wrinkled her nose again. "I thought people from the country were supposed to be hospitable. You didn't even offer your aunt a drink of water."

Lynette stood up again. "I'm sorry, Aunt Susan. Would you like something to drink?"

She was immediately waved off. "No thank you. Again, I won't be staying long."

"So typical." Lynette thought.

Her aunt continued. "I heard that you were moving to North Carolina so I wanted to come here to offer you a word of advice."

Lynette's eyes narrowed. "And what advise do you have to offer me today?"

"Take that child away from here and never look back."

Lynette was momentarily stunned. "I'm sorry?"

"You heard me. I said to take that child and run and never look back. There is nothing for you here."

"Why do you care so much? You've never been too keen to be around us."

Susan looked toward the house. "I will admit that I haven't visited often but you have to understand that I have a lot of obligations that need my attention on a daily basis. It's almost impossible to get away."

"Well it would have been nice to not be treated like a piece of gum on your shoe." Lynette replied quietly.

Both grew quiet for a moment before Susan broke the silence. "I apologize for that but you have to understand that it has been very difficult for me to come here since your mother died. This place used to be beautiful but now everything is in shambles. It's hard for me to look at." She then shook her head as if trying to shake away the memories. "Anyway, most of your brothers and sisters are morons. Half think they know everything and the other half really don't know a damn thing. Your daddy's the ring-leader. Don't think that I don't know what's been going on between all of you." Susan puffed out her bosom. "I'm the one who gave Rita the money to get you out of jail."

Lynette looked at her shocked. "You? Why would you do that? Who told you?"

"It doesn't matter who told me, and despite everything that has happened between us over the years, you are still my big sister's child and what happened to you and your child was wrong. I usually don't get into those type of affairs, of course, but I felt I needed to do something to help your situation; no matter how small."

Lynette smiled. "It wasn't small, Aunt Susan. I couldn't do anything for my baby sitting in jail. You have to let me pay you back."

"Nonsense. I am more than equipped to have handled your situation financially. Use your money for a better purpose." Susan lightly patted Lynette on the thigh. "Well I'm glad you both are together again as you should be. Your daughter is extremely intelligent and a very creative child. I would hate to see her mental and emotional growth stunted by.....” Susan looked around. “...unsavory surroundings. Just remember not to listen to stupidity or grow weak and you’ll be just fine.”

“I’ve already made up my mind so there’s no turning back now.”

Susan stood up. “Well, I’m not going to hold you up. It’s getting late and you’ve probably got a chicken to behead or a goat to milk so I’d better be going.” She briskly walked back to the car while her niece looked on.

“Bye Aunt Susan. Thank you for stopping by and also for the advice.” Lynette called after her and watched as the car slowly pulled away.

“Too late to milk that goat so I’d better start supper.” Lynette laughed to herself and walked towards the house humming.

*****

“Netty, get the phone! I’m trying to get some rest around here! Who’s calling so damn early anyway?”

Lynette who had been watering flowers on the back porch, ran inside to catch the phone before it stopped ringing. “Daddy, this makes no sense. You could have gotten the phone!” She picked it up quickly. “Hello?”

A somber voice answered on the other end. “Lynette, it’s me Diane.”

Lynette sighed. “Girl what are you doing calling so early?” She glanced at the clock which read 7:30 am. “I didn’t even think you got out of bed before noon.”

There was a pause on the other end.

“Diane?” Lynette was suddenly nervous. “Diane, what’s wrong? You’re scaring me. Is it Ms. Rose?”

Diane sniffled. "No, it's Eddie."

"Well spit it out for God's sake! You're scaring me. Is he in jail? Because I'm not touching a dime of my money to get him out?"

"My brother's dead." Diane stated matter-of-factly.

Lynette almost dropped the phone. "What do you mean dead? How? When? I don't understand." Her knees were getting weak so she sat down. "I'm so sorry, Diane. I don't know what to say." All she could think about was how this news could be broken to Ayanna. Her daughter had already been through enough but Lynette couldn't figure out a way to protect her from this kind of pain.

"They found him washed up by the James River shot in the head!" Diane shouted. "What kind of monster would do that? Eddie made plenty of mistakes but he didn't deserve this. I can't believe this is happening to my family. Not like this."

Lynette closed her eyes. "I don't know what to think right now. I've got to figure out a way to break this to Ayanna which isn't going to be easy. How's your mama? I can't even imagine how she must be feeling."

"Not good at all, girl. Evelyn is sitting with her now. Mama fainted when she heard the news; couldn't go down to identify the body so Evelyn did it."

"Damn. I'm so sorry. Police know anything?" Lynette asked even though she doubted they would ever find out who killed Eddie.

Diane sighed. "Of course not. This is Richmond. Who knows how many people got dragged out of the river and we'll never know how they got there. Listen. I just wanted to let you know what happened to Eddie. We've got to make these funeral arrangements and as soon as I get the day and time, I will let you know. Okay?"

"Of course, Diane. Let me know if there is anything I can do. I mean it."

She could hear Diane smile. "Thanks. I know you do. I will talk to you later and please take care of my niece."

"I always do. Talk to you soon." Lynette placed the phone down gently, and, with a heavy heart, allowed the tears to fall for the father of her child.

*****

The funeral was just a small gathering of family and friends. It was a cold windy day that dampened everyone's mood even more. No one could really wrap their minds around the events leading up to Eddie's death. To not know that someone they loved was so far gone and they didn't know about it was unimaginable. Eddie had not always been secretive when it came to his private life, but as he tunneled deeper and deeper into his addiction, his separation from his family and long-time friends had become more apparent. Everyone who attended carried their own brand of guilt. Each one feeling that they shared some part in Eddie's demise.

Ayanna was in a daze as she sat in front of her father's casket and barely heard the funeral director's last kind words as Eddie was lowered into the ground. She had been too angry to cry. Too shocked to make a sound. But when the casket was finally lowered into the ground, all of her emotions ran from her body, as she leaned over with tears spilling uncontrollably. The sob started deep within her soul and she felt as if she couldn't get enough air in her lungs. No sound would come out until it finally surfaced and the wail that escaped Ayanna's lips was a voice that she didn't recognize. She was barely conscious of her mother's arms that suddenly engulfed her in a crushing embrace, was barely aware of her brother doing his best to keep his own emotions together; more than aware of the fact that he had to be strong for his little sister.

"Lynette, we need to get these children away from the gravesite. It's not good for them to stay here."

This came from Diane who was holding up surprisingly well. She had made a promise to herself that she would not let herself give in to her heartache until she was in the privacy of her own home.

"I know. Come on baby, let's get out of here." Lynette spoke soothingly to her daughter. Then she turned to Sheila. "Why don't we get the kids out of here and head over to the re-pass? They don't need to be around all these people crying."

Sheila shook her head in agreement before blowing her nose in a handkerchief.

"Are you going to be okay?" Lynette asked.

"Yes. I'll be fine. This is all just so unreal to me."

"Well we've got to be strong for our children right now. Remember that." Lynette wondered what Eddie ever saw in this weak woman who stood in front of her. "Her own son is acting stronger than she is."

The four of them walked together, heading back to their vehicles. Along the way came condolences from all directions. Lynette accepted them on behalf of Ayanna and Cedric so they wouldn't have to say anything in response. Sheila just sniffled and covered her nose with her handkerchief while remaining silent. Everyone was headed to Eddie's mother Rose's home where the re-pass was being held. Upon arrival, Ayanna's spirits lifted when she saw all of the delicious food and her cousins calling for her from the kitchen. Mia and Anita's giggling was infectious as Kaley grabbed Ayanna's hand and dragged her over to the waiting duo.

"Hey Ayanna. You doing alright? I mean you know...." Mia shifted from side to side.

Ayanna blew out her breath. "Yeah. I'm doing alright. Cedric's been keeping me company a lot. Thanks for asking." She looked over and saw Anita trying to suppress a smile. "What's so funny anyway? You two were cracking up when I came in."

Mia looked over towards one of the older women fussing over a casserole. "That mean woman over there standing by grandma Rose. She started shouting at your dad's funeral. Remember?"

Ayanna started smiling. "Yeah, I remember."

Anita spoke up. "Well her wig fell to the side and has been hanging there ever since. Nobody's even bothered to tell her!" All four girls burst out laughing causing sharp stares from the older women before they went back to fussing over the food.

"I can't believe grandma didn't say anything. Watch everybody talk about her hair hanging on when she leaves." They started laughing again and were told to go somewhere else until the food was ready.

"I can't believe I was able to actually laugh today. I'm glad I've got great cousins."

Lynette had kept a watchful eye on Ayanna and was very pleased to hear her daughter's laughter from the other room. It meant everything to her to see her happy. She saw Ayanna and her three cousins run past her, grab Cedric, and run out the door with him protesting. She chuckled to herself and marveled at her daughter's resilience. You could never keep her down for long. It's as if her DNA makeup wouldn't allow for prolonged sadness and anger. She only wished that she possessed a portion of that characteristic.

She had been listening to Sheila go on and on about how terrible a person she used to be and how she had given herself over to God. She had accepted all apologies for any hostility shown to her by Sheila when Lynette and Eddie had dated briefly. Would Lynette please forgive her for how she treated her when she was pregnant with Ayanna? Lynette couldn't care less about her past conflicts with Sheila. She told her repeatedly that it was 'water under the bridge' and all was forgiven. When Sheila was finally convinced, she launched into a tirade of the dangers of drugs and how detrimental they could be. Thankfully, Lynette was saved when someone yelled that the food was ready and everyone made a dash for the kitchen. Rose had to fuss for the children to slow down and not make a mess. The men stood aside and chatted while the women and children made their plates first then sat down in various places to continue to discuss the events of the day. Evelyn sat down beside Lynette on the couch in the den.

"How are you doing?"

Lynette looked at Evelyn. "I should be asking you that. I'm sorry you had to lose your brother to such nonsense."

Evelyn fought back tears. "I know. But we all knew he was sick. It was just the way he was found." Evelyn shook her head. "I can't do this right now. I don't know how Diane is doing this. She's like a rock."

Both looked over in Diane's direction who was at the moment sitting with one of the elder women. Lynette noticed the strained look on Diane's face but didn't comment about it.

"So are you ready for your new life?" Evelyn asked.

"Am I? Are you kidding me? I'm more than ready. This situation we're in right now just confirms the fact that me and Ayanna need to make a fresh start. Everything's been arranged and we are set to go at the end of the school year."

Evelyn's eyes widened. "That's right around the corner, Lynette. Make sure you give me your information so I can keep in touch with you and my niece. I don't want us drifting apart like before." She grabbed Lynette's hand and squeezed. "You're a great mom and don't let anyone tell you otherwise."

Lynette smiled. "Thanks, Evelyn. I appreciate that. Especially since I don't get to hear it very often. And don't worry, before we leave, I'll make sure you have all my new information." She looked around the room. "For now, you just make sure you heal and keep an eye on Diane. She's not as tough as she looks."

"You're right and I will. Ayanna's probably going to need you a lot too."

"She's already got me and she knows it. Ayanna will be just fine."

Evelyn sighed and stood up slowly. "Well let me go make my rounds and talk to everybody."

Lynette looked up and smiled. "Do what you've got to do. I'm going to sit here and finish this pasta salad before I get me some of that homemade pound-cake.

Evelyn laughed. "I know that's right. Alright girl."

"Alright girl. I'll talk to you." She watched as Evelyn walked away.

Well, I can't believe it ended this way. But at least I know that we can move on from this and go on with our lives. Turns out this family isn't so bad and I actually wish I had let Ayanna get to know them sooner than now. Anyway, I can't change the past but I can at least be more open-minded about her family in the future. There's no way I can deny them to her. She loves them too much and they definitely love her. We'll make it work because I know we can do this. I just know it.

A New Beginning

Lynette was trying to hurry and finish packing the last of her and Ayanna's belongings before the moving truck arrived. She had managed to get her childhood friends, Chauncey and Leroy, to help with the move and drive. By offering them money for food, gas, and bus tickets back home, she had been assured that the move would go smoothly. Everything had fallen into place and it was time to leave the old life behind. Her thoughts turned to her father.

"Now gal you know you don't have to leave." Andrew stated solemnly.

Lynette, who had been taping up boxes, didn't bother to turn around. "I know I don't have to go, daddy, but I need to go. You and Jerome don't make it easy to live here; that's for sure."

"I know what I did was wrong. I don't know what got a hold of me."

"I really don't want to get into this with you. What's done is done. You thought what you were doing was right but you did it in the worst kind of way." She spun around to face Andrew. "And you did it to me! I'm the one who's always coming to your aid."

Andrew stepped forward. "I'm sorry, baby." He whispered.

Tears rolled down Lynette's face. "I know you are and I forgive you. I have to so I can move on."

They embraced and Andrew held on for a just a moment longer not willing to let his daughter go just yet.

Lynette smiled. "I love you too, daddy."

"So, you really leaving huh?"

Lynette turned around slowly to find Jerome standing in the doorway. "What do you want? You just don't know when to quit do you?"

Jerome smacked his lips. "You'll be back." He simply said and walked away.

Exhaling slowly, Lynette turned back to packing boxes. She perked up, however, when she heard Ayanna running through the back door.

"Mama, where are you?"

"Back here in the den!"

Ayanna appeared in the room like a whirlwind. "Hi ma! I got all my stuff together and everything's all packed except for my bathroom stuff." She said out of breath.

"Well were you running around the place the whole time?" Lynette laughed and reached out to hug her daughter. "Good baby. I'm done too. The only thing we're waiting on now is the truck."

Both went outside under the weeping willow to wait on Chauncey and Leroy who were both always late. Lynette didn't have time for that today, however. She had places to go. Besides, she was compensating them well enough that they should be on time for once. Ayanna was talking Lynette's ear off when she saw Rita's Volvo come flying around the curve and then crunching on the gravel in the driveway. She hadn't seen her best friend in about a month because she was busy getting prepared for her move, and hadn't realized just how much she missed her.

"Netty! Netty!" Rita called even before she could get her door fully open. "You know you can't go nowhere without saying goodbye." She tried to run as fast as she could to hug Lynette who took mercy on her and met her halfway.

"You know damn well I would never leave you without saying goodbye. What' wrong with you?"

Rita shook her head; tears streaming down her face. "I don't know what I'm going to do with you and my god-baby a whole state away. Damn! Can't you just move to Williamsburg or something? That's not too close where your family can mess with you."

Lynette smiled and wiped one of her friend's tears away. "Yeah, it's not that close but it ain't far away enough either. Now stop that crying before you make me cry."

"Hi Rita!" Ayanna ran over and gave her godmother a tight hug. "I'm going to miss you a lot. You know that don't you?"

"Oh you know I'm going to miss you too baby? I don't know why your old mean mama taking you away from me anyway." Rita started crying again.

Ayanna just squeezed her tighter. "Don't worry. I will make sure I come visit." She whispered.

"As much as you can?"

"I promise."

Suddenly, a loud horn blared. Chauncey was behind the wheel grinning from ear to ear and Leroy was hanging out the window smoking a cigarette. "Hey! What's going on my people? We here and we almost on time!" Leroy shouted.

"I guess you're right. Get on out of that truck so we can get this stuff loaded and get down this road." Lynette was already walking back to the house.

It took them just over one hour to load all of the items on the truck. Lynette had decided months ago that she was only going to take a few pieces of furniture including their bedrooms. She planned on buying everything new once moved into the new place and she could finally decorate the way she wanted.

As they were coming out of the house from doing their last-minute checks, a voice called out. "Excuse me. Everyone turned in the direction of the voice. "Do you remember me? I'm Olivia Rey...."

"I remember you Ms. Reynolds, of course. What do you want now? All that BS was cleared already so why don't just leave us alone?" Lynette brushed past her heading towards the truck.

The social worker cleared her throat and shifted uncomfortably. "Ms. Lee, please stop. I assure you that I'm not here to take away your daughter." She looked at the small group glaring at her. "Do you mind if I speak to you in private for a moment?"

Chauncey nudged Leroy. "Come on man. Let's make sure everything's secure in the back of the truck so we can get out of here. You come on too Yani." He narrowed his eyes at Olivia who shrunk back a little. "You good, Netty?'

"Yeah. Go on and I'll be done here in a minute." Lynette turned her attention back to Olivia. "I don't have much time. What do you want?"

"Well first I just wanted to check on Ayanna and make

sure that she's doing alright despite all of what she's been through."

Lynette looked over at her daughter by the truck laughing at something Chauncey was saying. "Yes, she's doing really good and she'll be doing much better once we get out of here."

Olivia smiled. "Yes. I noticed the truck when we pulled up. I'm very happy for you both."

Lynette didn't know if she had heard correctly. "I'm sorry. Did you say we pulled in?"

The smile dropped from Olivia's face. "Yes. That is the second reason I'm here. Since I was already familiar with your case, I was asked to accompany the authorities."

"Authorities? What are you talking about?" Then Lynette saw them. Two police cars parked by the side of the road. She didn't see anyone in the cars. "What's going on Ms. Reynolds?"

Olivia paused for a beat before she spoke. "The State released your daughter because it found no negligence on your part as her mother. You have maintained a steady job, and it is very evident that Ayanna isn't anywhere near neglected when it comes to food or clothing. Ayanna was very forthcoming about how much time is spent between you and her father's family. But this you already know. What you don't know is that Ayanna inadvertently started an entirely new investigation."

"How is that?" Lynette interrupted.

"When Ayanna was in the State's facility, she went to one of the councilors hoping to clear your name. She thought that she was taken away from you because of an altercation apparently between you and your brother that she intervened in. She was trying to protect you?" Olivia didn't wait for an answer. "She went on to tell us about the abuse that was going on in this home. There was nothing that could be done within our agency so we alerted the authorities. They asked us to assist since the child resided in the home with your brother. We assisted with obtaining the countless police records of 911 calls being placed and then no charges pressed. We know about the bruises on your father from hospital records. We were also able to gather information from some of your neighbors which wasn't easy, let me tell you."

Lynette could hardly speak. "You did this all because my baby came forward."

Olivia smiled. "That and your father assisting us too."

Lynette put her hands on her hips. "What? My daddy would never turn against his son."

"Yes, but apparently he loves his grand-daughter more. He kept saying that people got inside his head." Olivia looked toward the police cars. "In any event, those police officers are here to arrest your brother. I'm really sorry but we had no choice but to turn in our findings."

Lynette threw up her hands. "No. No. I understand. I just want my daddy to be okay."

At that moment, there was shouting heard from the woods. "Get your damn hands off me! What's this about?"

Jerome and the two police officers, flanked on each side of him, came storming out of the woods. Jerome just kept screaming obscenities and demanding what they were doing on his property. He stopped when he spotted his sister and Olivia standing together. "You think you've got the last laugh, don't you?" Jerome growled at Lynette.

"I don't think anything. But you've got to admit this is funny as hell."

Olivia chuckled discreetly and then covered her mouth with the back of her hand.

"You think this is funny!" Jerome shouted.

One of the police officers pulled out his cuffs. "Sir, please place your hands behind your back."

"No! I'm not doing a damn thing!"

Lynette and Olivia decided to quickly walk away at that moment while a scuffle ensued behind them. Lynette nodded goodbye to Olivia and hugged Rita again who headed back over to her brother. Lynette got in her car with her daughter by her side and honked at her friends to let them know she was ready to go.

"You ready baby?" She asked Ayanna softly.

Her daughter gave a wide smile. "Oh yeah. I'm ready."

Lynette squeezed her hand and turned around in time to see her brother getting handcuffed. Jerome must have felt her looking at him because he raised his head and turned briefly in her direction. As their eyes met, Lynette simply put a grin on her face and waved goodbye.

THE END